INV/03

LOVABLE
VALUABLES

LOVABLE VALUABLES

•

Veronica Kegel-Coon

AVALON BOOKS
NEW YORK

This book is dedicated especially to my dear friend,
Joyce Swanger and her husband, Rick Swanger,
whose real life love story inspired the
characters and plot of this novel.

And to my husband, Robert J. Coon,
and my son, Robby Coon,
who both make up the current of wind beneath my wings.

Chapter One

"**I**'m a collectible toy dealer, and I know what I'm talking about!" Joy shouted into the phone, wiping the August sweat from her brow before slamming down the receiver.

Her face now matched her bright red hair, which she pushed off her shoulders. She did not like to get so angry, but that insurance man really annoyed her. She hung up just as she heard the shop bell ring. She looked up and waved to Mrs. Kellerman, who was walking through the door holding the hand of her granddaughter, Melissa.

"Hi there," Joy called, with a wave of her hand.

"Rough day, Joy?" Mrs. Kellerman asked, raising her eyebrow.

"No, I just got off the phone with the most an-

1

noying insurance agent. He refuses to believe that a 1962 Ronnie doll is worth eight thousand dollars," she said, pointing to the glass case in the front of the shop. "The client who requested I sell those dolls has died of cancer, and she wanted all the proceeds to go to the Cancer Foundation."

Mrs. Kellerman nodded. Joy put her hands on her hips and looked around her shop. She was sure one could probably still read *Joy's Lovable Collectibles* through the dirty window, but she wanted everyone to notice the Captain Midnight toys displayed there. She didn't think the windows and cases had been cleaned since her ex-boyfriend had left her for another woman.

"You mean Mrs. Michaels's dolls, right?" Mrs. Kellerman's eyes lit up with interest. "I did hear that you had her entire collection for sale."

Joy looked over at Melissa, who was peering into the large doll case at the porcelain dolls. She noticed the smile on the child's face and meandered to the back of the store to join her.

"So, it's Melissa's birthday soon, right?" Joy's bright blue eyes twinkled with enthusiasm as she clapped her hands. Her dangling turquoise earrings shook as she moved her head.

"That's right, Joy, you guessed it," Mrs. Kellerman said. "Melissa decided she wanted to come here to pick out her present. Are all of Mrs. Michaels's old Ronnie dolls back there?" Mrs. Kellerman asked.

"Well, the two most valuable ones are in the display case at the front of the shop right below the cash register. I've got to lock them up at night in the vault since they're so rare." Joy smoothed her long blue peasant skirt.

The cash register sat on top of a floor display case with a glass panel. Joy always put her current favorite collectibles there since that case usually caught the customer's eye first. Right now, she needed to find a spot for the Daddle toys.

"I was so sorry to hear about Mrs. Michaels's death. I always liked her, but felt sorry for her. She suffered so much at the end," Mrs. Kellerman said, shaking her head slowly. "Her husband died young, she couldn't have children, and then she died so tragically. Oh well, I guess money can't buy everything, huh?"

Before Joy could nod her head, Melissa blurted, "So how'd she get cancer?"

"Look at the Ronnie dolls, dear," Mrs. Kellerman said, patting her granddaughter's hand.

"Yes, please do," Joy added, trying to help Mrs. Kellerman change the subject.

Mrs. Kellerman and Melissa moved to the front of the shop and stood in front of the case looking at two old Ronnie dolls with pageboy hairstyles in black sheath dresses.

Joy liked chatting with Melissa about the dolls. It made her feel as though she was an expert at something, even though that expertise didn't always pay her bills month to month. Suddenly, the bell over the door rang, and she turned her head to see a handsome man in a navy blue pinstripe suit step inside.

He was tall and broad, with black hair graying at the temples. His neatly trimmed mustache also had flecks of gray in it. He paused for only a moment before moving toward the large electric train case next to the front window. Then he slowly took out a camera from his pocket. Joy watched him, wondering what he was doing here in the middle of the day. He looked like he should be seated in a downtown law office.

She was about to ask him if he needed help when he turned to her and said, "Hello, Ms. Smathers. I'm the one you were talking to earlier. I'd really like to see these Ronnie dolls that are worth such an obscene amount of money."

Joy blushed immediately, remembering how rude she had been on the phone. She bit her lower lip, then smiled sheepishly. "Oh yes, how nice. Well, I'm sorry I shouted. You see, someone was running a vacuum cleaner earlier, and it was so hard to hear over the noise." She didn't like to fib, but it seemed to be working so she continued pleasantly, "I have no help here as you can see, so I have to do two things at once, and as I recall you were questioning the value of those two beauties I have in the doll case over there. The ones Melissa's looking at right now."

As she spoke, she nodded her head in the little girl's direction then moved closer to the door. Mrs. Kellerman turned around with a puzzled frown. *What a day to insult an insurance man!*

"Oh, I see." He grinned and moved toward the case with his camera ready to take a picture. "I must say, I thought you were really annoyed with me. Buckley and Voucher Insurance doesn't insure too many dolls worth eight thousand dollars. I felt I just had to come down here and take a look for myself," he explained, as he snapped a picture of the two Ronnie dolls.

"Naturally." Joy smiled. She noticed there was a real sparkle in his deep dark eyes. "By the way, I'm sorry, but I didn't catch your name earlier."

"Rich Buckley," he said, extending a hand to her as he stepped forward. "You know I'm really glad to know you didn't deliberately hang up on me."

He was laughing as he spoke and Joy tried to giggle along with him. It seemed hard to imagine this genteel man upsetting her as much as he had earlier.

"I really am sorry if I sounded rude. We'll talk later, after I've helped this lady and her granddaughter." She then turned back to Mrs. Keller-man and Melissa as Rich Buckley nodded his head. "Melissa, honey, have you decided?"

She watched him move back to the train case from the corner of her eye. He was looking inside with keen interest.

"I think I want her," Melissa said, pointing to an old 1976 Ronnie doll with a frizzy hairdo. The price tag was two hundred dollars. "I really like her. She's got a super cool look." The child's freckled face smiled when she spoke.

"Very well, then. The frizzy-haired Ronnie doll it shall be." Joy extracted the keys from her skirt pocket and opened the glass case.

But she couldn't take her eyes off the man standing in the corner. She wondered what he was feeling when he looked at those old trains. Old toys evoked such a wide array of emotions in people.

"I really love these old Ronnies. I play with them all the time," Melissa said.

"So did I when I was your age, honey," Joy said to Melissa. Then, turning to Mrs. Kellerman she asked, "Will there be anything else?"

The older woman nodded. "Yes, I want that antique porcelain doll with the red hair, as well. She'll look nice in my curio cabinet. Oh, when's the doll show?"

"Next week. I'm hoping I'll get a buyer for those two Ronnies." Joy closed the doll case slowly. "Now, Mrs. Kellerman, I'll be spending a lot of time trying to figure out which collectibles will catch your eye next time. Tell me you're going to buy another curio cabinet, right?"

Mrs. Kellerman laughed. Joy noticed Mr. Buckley looking their way.

"Don't worry. You'll never lose me as a customer," the older woman said as Joy handed her the doll. "Just put that on my tab."

Joy nodded and moved back to the register. The total sale was $1,000.00 and had made her day a profitable one. Now she could tell Mom she might be able to pay all her bills this month.

"Mrs. Kellerman, I'm lucky to have good customers like you. You make my efforts worthwhile." She tossed her hair back with the shake of her head again. "Enjoy that old doll, Melissa. You're lucky to have a nice grandmother who buys you genuine antiques."

Melissa waved good-bye as they left. Joy then folded her arms across her chest and walked slowly to the front display case. Rich Buckley turned to face her and their eyes locked for a lingering moment.

"So, do you also do appraisals?" he asked, trying to fill the silent space between them.

"Yes, I do, and you're probably wondering why these two Ronnie dolls are worth eight thousand dollars a piece, aren't you?" Standing with her arms crossed under her chest, she leaned against the display case, deliberately blocking his view.

He put his hands in his pockets and said, "No, Ms. Smathers, I asked someone I know to verify the current list price for the first 1962 Ronnie doll, and she said your price was fair."

"Oh, so your wife's a doll collector."

"No," he replied slowly after a pregnant pause. "I'm not married."

She noted the disturbed look on his face when he answered that question. What was that about? She then lightened her tone of voice. "Gee, how does a guy like you manage to stay single?" She leaned back and smiled at him again.

"Oh, easily. But what I really want to know is, how old are the trains in this case? Are they the really old metal trains?"

"Yep, before the electric motors," Joy piped up, noting the fascinated look on his face. She could tell he was revisiting his youth now. She loved to see that faraway look on her customers' faces.

"I had a set of those trains a long, long time ago," he said, laughing. He jingled the change in his trouser pocket and took a step back. "I forgot about them. I can't even remember what my parents did with that set that I had."

His eyes glowed when he smiled. Joy thought she felt her heart melting inside her chest.

"So, Mr. Buckley, it appears you do have at least one other interest in life besides insurance—somehow I imagined you being a total workaholic." She nervously pushed back her unruly red mane as she spoke. "You sounded so serious about the policy when I spoke to you on the phone. I always think of men like you being driven by their work."

"And you seem to have one all-consuming passion for toys, I see. And by the way, you should really call me Rich," he said. "We insure a lot of small businesses like yours, but we don't insure such high quality small items. I didn't mean to sound like I was giving you a hard time." He scratched his neck. "My partner's been working like the dickens to cover larger business clients." He smiled. "You've really got a unique shop here."

"Well, I like the unusual." She wondered what he meant by the last remark. "I've always loved old toys, and I wanted my own shop to be full of them. . . . so here I am. Several members of my family—like my mother—think I'm nuts, but what can I say?"

Their eyes met again. The intensity of his gaze was enough to knock her over. She felt her cheeks flush again. Why hadn't she put on more make-up this morning before coming downstairs to the shop? She watched Rich Buckley take out a small pad and pen from his suit pocket and jot down some notes.

"Well, I'm impressed, Ms. Smathers. I'd heard about your shop, but I never really thought to come take a look."

"Oh, call me Joy," she said, touching the folds of her long peasant skirt nervously. "So you just came down here to check out the Ronnie dolls?"

He laughed. "Yes, but now I know I'll have to come down here more often. Your place is fascinating. You know, I haven't seen Magic toys in years. It's amazing that something you spend so much time with in your youth can end up being worth so much money."

She shook her head. "Things that bring back memories usually end up being of great value to someone."

"What's that train set worth?" he asked, staring into the display case as he spoke.

"Well, that set right there's selling for one thousand dollars." She wished she could climb into the case so he could stare at her.

"Really? Well, I guess that just proves what my grandmother used to say: if you hold onto something long enough, eventually it's worth money."

She laughed. "Good old grandmothers always know the truth about those things, don't they?

Mine used to say things like, 'don't throw away your gold.' "

"Yeah, well, I don't mean durable value." He cleared his throat and Joy felt nervous with the sudden change in his tone. "I mean, the things you have in this shop are interesting and all that, but their worth isn't going to increase if the economy goes south."

"What's that supposed to mean?" She put her hands on her hips, aware that her stance was a defensive one. "Come on now, life's too short. If everyone put money aside for financial security, what fun would they ever have in their lives? Different things hold different values for people. People who buy things in this shop are collectors; they collect for a variety of reasons, and to add some sort of increased quality to their lives."

He put his pen and pad back into his pocket and stared at her.

"I think my customers believe in enjoying their lives a bit," she continued as she paced the floor. "Oh, sure, I get a few serious investors every now and then, but most of the collectors I know do it for fun."

"Ah, I see. So most of your loyal fans pay these outrageous prices just to have fun." He grinned and clasped his hands behind his back.

"Don't you ever buy something cute or silly just for fun?" She looked directly at him when she asked him this question. It had been a long time since she had been intrigued by a man—she wanted an answer. She took a step closer to him, crossed her arms and asked in a low husky voice, "So what do you do for fun, sir?"

She wanted him to laugh, but he looked at her with a straight poker face and said, "I play golf in my spare time."

"For business or for pleasure?" she asked, shaking her head.

He looked away from her, obviously uncomfortable. She was surprised to see this strong reaction.

"Well, I do it for both reasons, really. Why?" he asked defiantly.

Joy softened her tone of voice as she backed down. "Nothing. I just always think of golf as the game rich businessmen play to clinch deals, not to relax. That's all."

"Just what makes you so sure I'm rich?" he asked.

"You have a distinguished air about you. Come on, now. You have your own insurance company. Your suits are worth more than my sofa. What else can I say? You don't hide your success."

He swallowed and said, "I see."

"I *can* tell something about your past, though," she said, moving closer to him and looking directly into the case.

"Oh, so you tell fortunes too?" he asked, laughing, raising an eyebrow as he looked at her.

She grinned. "I can tell that at one time in your life, trains were your primary obsession, and once upon a time you really knew how to lose yourself in something. Was that so very long ago?"

"Way back when, before I got too big for my britches so to speak."

"Ah, when you were a small boy. Shouldn't you unleash the child in you again, Rich? How many trains do you remember?"

He paused and scratched his chin for a moment. "Not many. I just remember the huge platform my dad had built for me, and we used to play with those trains for hours. I also remember I had another set later on. I think it was right before the first G size train came out."

"Mm, sounds about right, chronologically," she replied.

He stared at her with a puzzled expression on his face. "Those trains did come out after the Hassel trains did, and they were all the rage for awhile. I guess you really have to have lots of historical knowledge to run this sort of shop."

"People pay me for my expertise, sir. But I bet you know about as much about toy trains as I do." She moved her head in the direction of the window as she spoke. His gaze was too intense for her.

"So, how did you get to know Mrs. Michaels?" he asked, changing the subject.

Her jaw dropped. How did he know the dolls were from her collection?

Chapter Two

Rich Buckley just smiled at her. He didn't like to think about Mrs. Michaels. The solitary, eccentric doll collector had been a member of his country club for years.

"Her dolls were all she had at the end of her life," Joy answered, knitting her eyebrows together.

"Yeah, I know," he said. "I knew her from the country club, and she wasn't a very happy woman. She was nice, but never happy." He cleared his throat but did not take his eyes off her as she moved.

The unusual redhead standing before him seemed to have such gusto and passion for life.

Her eyes sparkled with enthusiasm, just like Margie's had when he'd first met her.

"She also lent me the money to start this shop," she said softly, and he noticed that she looked as if she was struggling not to cry. Was the memory of Loretta Michaels so painful to her?

"By the way, if you don't mind my asking, how *did* you get started?" he asked, taking a step closer to the counter.

"Well, gee, that's a really long story. I always loved collectible toys, and one day I met a wealthy collector with lots of dolls whose children were grown. Mrs. Michaels not only lent me the money to start this shop, but also paid for the shop's publicity for three years."

His eyes drank in the sight of this lovely woman with the flaming red hair. She probably knew things about these trains that he'd always wanted to know. He was so busy looking at her that he didn't hear the knock on the shop window. He saw Joy turn her head to the window and wave to a tall blond woman with bobbed hair who was holding a brown bag up to the window. Joy looked back at her and winked an eye. The woman then turned her blond head to Rich with keen interest.

"Oh, that's my friend, Cassie. She owns the flower shop next door," Joy said.

"How nice. Looks like she's got something for you."

"She's got our four o'clock coffee, either café latté or cappuccino."

"Well, since I wasn't invited to this social gathering, I'd better go," he said pleasantly. "I've probably spent too much of my afternoon here already."

As Cassie pushed the door open, Joy began to talk.

"Cassie, this is Rich Buckley from the insurance company. He's not here to charm me, just to look the store over—you know, for policy purposes."

She giggled as she spoke, but stopped when she realized neither were laughing. Rich was cursing the moment because he'd wanted to talk to her more about those trains. He liked her sense of humor. His ex-wife Margie had once had such a sense of humor.

"I'm Cassie Fisher." Cassie extended her free hand to Rich and shook her head of fluffy hair.

Joy was still standing next to the counter, but he could see her lower lip was trembling. She looked so pretty standing there silently. Her friend kept smoothing her short blonde hair as she spoke to him.

"Mr. Buckley, I've heard so much about your

company. It's so exciting to meet you. You're Joy's friend?" asked the tall blond.

"Nope, just her insurer, really. I'm not sure she wants me as a friend," he said, laughing.

Cassie set down the brown bag. "What a shame—for Joy, I mean." Her voice was light and amusing.

Rich turned to go. "I think I'd better get back to the office. You ladies have a nice coffee break. It's certainly been fun, Ms. Smathers. I'll be sure to come again."

"Oh, thanks, Rich. I hope you do come again. And have a nice afternoon," Joy called after him as he walked out the door.

Did she really mean it? he wondered as he walked to his car. Maybe he could come back tomorrow on his lunch hour and talk some more. No, he shouldn't. She might think he was being too forward.

As he drove down Main Street to his office he wondered what she would be like as a dinner date—probably fascinating.

"Come on, Buckley, get real here," he muttered to himself. "You've only just met the woman."

He passed two kids riding bikes as he turned onto Swallow Street. He stopped to watch them. They were laughing as they rode by. Children always brought back the sad memory of his failed marriage.

"Margie, I love you so much, but our life isn't complete."

She lay on the four poster bed in her pink silk robe and shook her head. She bit a fingernail and then got up to pace the floor. She stopped at the doorway. Her dark hair hung loosely around her shoulders, but her back was turned to him.

"Rich, children would only get in the way. Can't you understand I'm happier without them? I'm shooting to become executive vice-president one day. I want to be the best."

His heart was ripping inside his chest. Why was his wife, the only woman he had ever loved, so career driven? He stood staring at the bed with his hands in his pockets.

"I always thought we wanted the same things. I want a family."

"Well, darling, if you were more ambitious, you could understand how I feel." Margie went back and sat on the bed. She was laughing at him. "A child does nothing but complicate your life."

"I told you when we were first married how important it was to me!" he roared. She just continued to laugh. "You just wanted my money and family connections to help your career, didn't you?"

"YOU! You didn't have as much money as

my family used to have. You only built this insurance company with the help of Joe Voucher. Your folks would never have been able to get into the country club since you haven't got much in the way of blue blood. My mother thought your folks were low class."

Margie glared at him. She lay back on top of the pillows and steepled her hands behind her head. Was this cold woman really the one he'd fallen in love with four years ago?

"Face it, Rich. The only reason someone with all I've got could be interested in someone like you was money. Who would you ever have married if I had said no? Would you really have settled for Caroline Voucher? Maybe she would've been a better choice for you, since she's so family oriented. She wouldn't notice how dull you are."

"What do you want from me? What have you ever wanted from me?" He was shaking in anger. He could hear his voice cracking.

"I want a more exciting life than I got!" Margie jumped up from the bed and stalked out of the room. "You're so boring! All you ever think about is your family, having babies, and your father's insurance company! You never want to go anywhere fun! You never cared about my hopes and dreams!"

"You're a workaholic, Margie," he called after her.

She walked back into the room a few seconds later. Her eyes were red from crying.

"I'm so ashamed. Our marriage is a sham!" She wiped her eyes on the back of her hand.

"Ashamed of me or of yourself?" He spun around to face her. "What's the point of this marriage?" He slammed his fist into the wall. "If you want to pursue material success to the hilt, go ahead. I won't stand in your way. You can have your divorce as soon as you want."

He was tempted to shake her, to make her realize love was more important than success. Instead, he just stood clenching his fists at his sides.

She shook her head and wept. "You're pathetic! I'll go, but don't blame me for what went wrong. Good-bye, Rich."

He felt needles piercing his heart. How could love go so wrong? What had he ever done to deserve such pain?

He could never forget how horrible that night had been. It all seemed like a terrible nightmare. He didn't like thinking about it, but he did. Now she was gone, and he couldn't feel anything

deeply anymore. Days just drifted by with no purpose, and life was incredibly dull without Margie.

Before walking into his office, he shook his
head and rubbed his temples. Would this hurt ever
go away?

Chapter Three

"Joy, I think it's time you forgot about Larson and started dating again," Cassie said, putting her coffee cup down on the counter top.

Joy rolled her eyes and took a sip of the steaming brew. "I must be addicted to coffee to drink it on a steaming hot day like this," she said with a deep sigh.

"So what's the scoop on the insurance guy? Is he married?" Cassie asked with a grin.

"No, Cass, and don't go getting any ideas. I don't even know the guy." Joy pulled up a wooden stool and sat down.

"He's gorgeous, Joy."

She was silent; she wanted to choose her words carefully. Cassie had made it her lifetime ambition to fix Joy up with the right man, since she was married to the perfect husband who supported her dream of owning her own flower shop.

She also didn't want to confide to Cassie that she had felt some odd force come over her when Rich Buckley had walked in today, and that she had found the feeling overwhelming.

"Cassie, the guy's got his own insurance company and belongs to the local country club for goodness sake. He's hardly my type."

"So you've never even seen him before?"

"No, of course not," Joy replied indignantly.

"Hmm, I call it strange fate if you ask me." Her friend took a long swallow of coffee.

"Cass, I'm not in the mood for your talk about destiny today."

Cassie pushed a lock of her hair behind her ear and raised her left eyebrow. Joy watched her friend for a moment thinking how annoying Cassie could be at times, though she was by far her dearest friend. Cassie had been the only other person who understood Joy's desperate need to have her own collectible toy shop.

"Joy, you can't keep reliving that awful relationship with Larson forever. The time's come for you to move on, my friend."

Joy let out a deep breath. Cassie had been married for so long she just didn't understand how hard it was to be single.

"So what has Larson got to do with Rich Buckley?"

"Nothing, but did Larson ever pay that phone bill he stuck you with?" Cassie asked. When Joy shook her head, Cassie added, "I thought not. What a loser." Joy just looked down at the floor, away from her friend. Her relationship with Larson had been one of the biggest disappointments in her life.

He had been an artist. She had supported him for years, thinking that one day they would be married. He was the only man she had ever been with and for whom she had compromised her ideals.

"Come on, Joy. Let's not feel sorry for ourselves here. I know this Mr. Buckley isn't your usual cup of tea, but he's fascinating and you know he'll come back into the shop."

"Cassie, you've been reading too many romance novels."

"He'll ask you out. I just know it."

"And what *is* my usual cup of tea, Cass?"

"The artistic loser type," Cassie snapped. "Face it, Joy, you pick guys who need to be taken care of. These artsy types you like aren't as stable as my Fred is, for example."

"Fred's an architect, Cass. That's pretty artistic if you ask me."

"You know what I'm saying."

Even though Joy was arguing with her best friend, she knew she needed to analyze her problems with men. Her friend had good insight.

"But my Fred has practical business sense," Cassie said pointing her index finger in the air. "*Both* sides of Fred's brain work—only one side of your boyfriends' brains work."

"Okay, so Larson was immature. I agree with you."

"Joy," Cassie said after a long pause. "I think you'd like me to fix you up with this Mr. Buckley character."

"Cassie, you're my dearest friend, and I love you. However, let's not get ridiculous."

"Joy, I'm not trysting with you today. Drink your coffee, and tell me how your day went. Say, I did see Mrs. Kellerman in here?"

"Yes, and she bought a thousand dollars worth of stuff."

Cassie let out a low whistle. "Wouldn't we all like to have that kind of money."

"I need more customers like her now that Mrs. Michaels is dead."

"Sure. Hey, Joy, are you busy Saturday night? Fred has this single friend, and—"

"Oh no, Cass, not another blind date, please."

Just then the phone rang. Joy jumped to her feet and grabbed the receiver from the wall.

"Hello, Joy's Lovable Collectibles," she said.

"Hello, Ms. Smathers, this is Rich Buckley."

"Oh, hi, Rich," she said enthusiastically, looking over to see Cassie almost drop her Styrofoam container. She then turned away from Cassie, facing the wall, so she wouldn't have to watch her friend's face.

"I know this is short notice, but I was just wondering . . . I thought maybe we could continue our conversation about those toy trains over dinner at my club."

"Club?" she asked nervously.

"My country club, I mean. I could pick you up in about an hour."

"Sure, I could be ready at seven," she answered, noting that her heart was pounding with excitement.

"And where's your place?" he asked.

"Rich, my apartment's right over the shop. The entrance is out back near the dumpster." She heard Cassie groan behind her.

"Great, see you in an hour."

Before she could put the receiver down, Cassie was jumping up and down. "He's taking you to the Applebloom Country Club? See, I was right!" She then slapped her forehead. "I better get out of here, Joy, so you can get ready."

"I can't believe I agreed to do this," Joy said in a low voice.

"I'm not even going to comment—it would just

lead to another intense discussion. Joy, I just want to remind you: all men are not like Larson. Please keep that in mind this evening."

Joy nodded her head as she watched her friend leave the store. She was disappointed Cassie didn't stay longer. She was all nerves right now, and her friend sometimes dispatched good advice.

She was about to lock up the shop when the phone rang again.

"Hello, dear," the high pitched voice squeaked.

"Hi Mom," she answered with a moan.

Joy could not tolerate her mother for long periods of time. She was always asking prying questions and berating Joy for not having a "real" profession.

"How many toys did you sell today, dear?"

Joy twisted the phone cord as she spoke. Making large knots with the cord seemed to ease the frustration she felt while talking to her mother. She paced back and forth behind the counter as she spoke.

"So, Mom, what's the latest gossip?" she asked as she chewed her lower lip.

"Well, I had to call and tell you that Pamela Rains and Harold Twin were seen together at the theater the other day night. Did you know everyone's saying she's the cause of his divorce? I wonder. . . ." Her mother paused.

"Yeah, well, what can I say?" Joy answered without interest, twirling a lock of hair around her finger. *Would she please hang up soon?*

"Really, Joy, if that Pamela can snatch a CEO like Harold Twin, then you should be able to find yourself a decent guy," her mother whined.

"Mother, let it go," Joy snapped, releasing her hair.

"I'm sorry, dear. I'm your mother, and I worry about you. You're almost thirty and still dating losers."

"I'm not thirty yet, Mom, and I have a good life."

"Look, dear, you need to join a singles' club. You can't live off overpriced toys your entire life. You don't want to be alone in your old age."

Joy clutched the phone tightly and looked up at the ceiling. *When would she cut this nonsense out?*

"You realize you haven't been on a date since last spring?"

Joy rolled her eyes again. "Well, Mom, I'm going out tonight, so I'd better go."

"I hope this one's better than that Larson character you ditched."

"Mom, he dumped *me*, remember?" Joy asked between clenched teeth. "I have to go."

It suddenly dawned on her that Rich Buckley

was exactly the sort of man her mother would approve of wholeheartedly—she should say as little as possible right now.

However, her mother's pace picked up, "So where did you meet this man? Did Cassie introduce you to him?"

"No, I just met him in the shop this afternoon," Joy said quickly. "I better hang up right now, but I promise I'll come over to see you one day next week. We can talk then."

Joy was just about to put the receiver back when her mother cried, "So what's his name, for Pete's sake?"

"Rich Buckley, of the Buckley and Voucher Insurance Company. Now, good-bye, Mom."

She then hung up the phone and let out a sigh of relief.

Chapter Four

"Well, Buckley, you did it. I guess you were checking out more than just the Ronnie dolls in that shop this afternoon." James Pyle turned off his computer and looked over at Rich, who had just hung up the phone.

"Yeah," he muttered. "I just, you know, wanted to talk about those toy trains some more. And I thought it might make some interesting dinner conversation." Rich rubbed the back of his neck and continued, "You should've seen those trains, James. And this woman was so odd, but interesting."

"Rich, if you're going to the club tonight, you'd better watch out. Your partner's daughter is going to be there with him, and you know she's got the hots for you." James chuckled and stood up.

Rich couldn't deny the fact that he wanted to see Joy Smathers again. Their talk had been so interesting, and it had rejuvenated him this afternoon. She reminded him of a gypsy girl with her long scarlet mane of hair and full figure (not like one of those skinny toothpicks at the club), and she spoke with such animation.

James looked at Rich and then slung his jacket over his shoulder. "You know, your partner's still pushing to move this office into the big city. Voucher's set on insuring big rig companies; he wants out of the Mom and Pop shops."

"Right, James, I'll talk to Joe later. I think it's too much expansion too soon."

James nodded. "Hey, have a nice time. I'm glad you're going out tonight. You know, I haven't seen you in such a pleasant mood since—"

"Since Margie left?" Rich interjected, finishing the sentence for him.

"You said it," James said, heading for the door. "Just avoid Joe and his daughter, Caroline, and you should have a good evening. I'll talk to you tomorrow."

Joy closed the shop early and went upstairs to her apartment. She greeted her cat, Igor, as she walked in the door.

The evening might bring something. This date was special, unlike the ones Cassie set up for her.

"Now the big question, Igor, what should I wear?"

She picked a lovely short cocktail dress in deep blue, then showered and fixed her hair and eye make-up. Then she rapidly made her bed and raced around straightening up the apartment. Surely, a man like Rich Buckley did not tolerate sloppiness.

Why was she so nervous? This guy was clearly out of her league, status-wise. They'd probably just have dinner tonight, and that would be it. That's all. Surely the differences between them would not be good for a long term relationship. He was so straight laced—the type who probably voted a straight Republican ticket in each election.

"Don't worry, Igor, you're not being replaced. This is simply a one night deal, that's all. And no, Igor, I'm not still hung up on Larson, despite what Cassie wants to think." Her cat meowed in response.

Just then the phone rang. She immediately ran to the kitchenette and answered, "Hello, Cassie."

"How'd you know it was me?" her friend asked.

"How could I not know, Cass? You always call to give me advice before a date."

"Well, I just want to warn you not to lose your

temper with him, no matter what he says. You tend to fly off the handle, Joy, and guys find that a real turnoff. So stay cool. Be your charming self, and have fun. You know it's been a while since you've gone out."

"Cass, I'll be fine, and now I've got to go. Talk to you tomorrow." She was about to hang up the receiver.

"See, Joy, there you go. You're sounding mad at me already. Remember, keep it cool."

"Cass, honestly, doesn't it ever occur to you and Mom that maybe, just maybe, I'm perfectly happy being single?" Joy snapped into the phone.

"Oh no you're not, Joy Smathers. You recently pinned all your hopes and dreams on the wrong man. Now that you've met an intriguing stranger, you've got to accept the fact that something just might happen here."

"Yeah, sure." Joy was silent for a moment, then hung up the phone. Had she simply imagined that something had clicked with her and Rich Buckley this afternoon?

A few minutes later the doorbell rang. As soon as she opened it, Igor hissed at Rich. He stood in the doorway with a bouquet of flowers in his hand, and he was grinning from ear to ear. But his grin diminished as Igor ran away, leaving tufts of white fur behind him.

"Well, I'm sorry I don't meet your cat's standard of approval," he said with a laugh.

"Igor's very shy with people he doesn't know. Come on in. These flowers are lovely. You really shouldn't have."

"No, I guess I should've brought fresh fish for your cat. Although I've always thought that lovely women deserve fresh flowers." She noticed that he was looking around the apartment at her secondhand re-upholstered furniture. "Say, nice place. I bet you decorated it yourself. It sure has your touch."

"Thanks. I'll just grab my purse and we'll go." Joy led him down the stairs after she locked the apartment door, noting the tension that hung in the air between the two of them.

"Do you own the whole building?" he asked, touching her arm lightly.

"No, I just rent the entire building."

After he opened the door to his Mercedes Benz for her, he casually asked her about the crime rate in the neighborhood.

"Nobody steals here that I know of, Rich," she replied.

"I'm just thinking of all those valuable toys you have inside. You've got a top line security system, right?"

"Are you asking as my insurer or as a concerned friend?" she asked as she slid into the front seat of the car.

"I guess I'm both," he answered as he started the engine.

They settled into comfortable conversation all the way to the country club. Joy had heard of the Applebloom Country Club and how exclusive it was. She took a deep breath of fresh summer air. The evening was perfect.

Rich could hear music playing inside the clubhouse as he opened the car door. The waltz tune that wafted down the drive sounded very romantic. It reminded him of days gone by. Margie had loved to dance to music like this. He noticed Joy seemed to be enjoying the soft sound of the delicate music.

He took her arm and led her through the grand hallway of the clubhouse. There were several couples dancing in each other's arms at the front of the ballroom.

"Would you like a drink?" he asked, thinking how lovely she looked in the blue dress. It complimented her hair and eyes perfectly.

"Sure. I'll have a mineral water," she answered.

"Well, I'll have the same," he told the waiter as he settled into his seat.

"Rich Buckley, *there* you are. I've been calling your office all day, and I left three messages." The loud, high-pitched voice shouted across the room.

Oh brother, it was Caroline. James had predicted she'd be here tonight. He turned to see Caroline in a short, white dress standing right next to his table. Her long blond hair was pulled back and showed her pearl earrings. She glanced over at Joy, then turned her eyes to Rich as if demanding an explanation.

"Hello, Caroline. I was very busy this afternoon and didn't get a chance to return any phone calls," he answered firmly.

She wailed, "You know Daddy was looking forward to playing golf with you this afternoon. You really should apologize to him—you know he does not like to be kept waiting."

"Yes, well, Caroline, I had a lot to do this afternoon. Oh, and allow me to introduce Joy Smathers." He turned his head in Joy's direction as he spoke. "Joy, this is Caroline Voucher. She's my partner's daughter."

"Hello. I'm also an old family friend. And just what do you do?" Caroline did not look at Joy as she spoke. Her eyes were still focused on Rich.

Joy answered with an awkward hello and sat back in her chair. Rich knew he had to get rid of Caroline fast—she could be very rude when she felt like it. Joy simply shook her head of long hair and leaned back in her chair.

"Caroline, Joy has a fantastic collectible toy shop downtown. You'd love her dolls. You know, she's a real expert on old toys. You just would not believe the things she has in her shop. Do you know she has an old cast iron train set selling for a fortune in this store of hers. She could tell you so much about those old Ronnie dolls you used to play with—"

"So she's a client," Caroline interrupted, nodding her head at Joy as if she weren't present.

"Yes, she's the client I was visiting this afternoon," Rich continued, ignoring Caroline's annoyance.

"Well Rich, I really am disappointed. I'd hoped we could talk more tonight. You know we have a club meeting later this week, and I really can't wait much longer."

Goodness gracious, would she ever quit? Why did she have to be here tonight?

"Caroline, we'll discuss your situation later in the week. Nothing needs to be decided today." He knew his voice was getting edgy now. "Joy, would you—"

"No, I just promised the client I'd talk with you today," she interrupted with a wail.

Joy was beginning to look uncomfortable with this insistent woman. Rich watched her swallow before she spoke up, "Rich, if you would like to discuss some business matter, I could always take a walk, or go to the ladies' room or something."

Darn, why did Caroline always succeed in getting her way?

"Caroline, Joy and I have come here together for the evening. Now, please, I'll get back to you later. Give your father my apologies." *Couldn't she take a hint?*

But Caroline only tried a different tactic. Rich watched her turn to Joy and smile. "Joy, are you the same dealer who's selling Loretta Michaels's doll collection?" Caroline asked, looking at Joy from the corner of her eye. Joy nodded in affirmation. "Well, then, I'll have to come into your shop sometime soon." She clapped her hands in front of her and showed her teeth in a broad grin. "Well, may the two of you have an enjoyable evening. Call me first thing tomorrow, Rich. Hopefully by then you'll be ready to discuss more important things than toys. And Rich, can you meet me here for lunch tomorrow?"

"No, I can't, but I'll get back to you." He nodded his head as he spoke, trying to mask his irritation with her tone of voice.

"And, Rich, I also need you to look at the muffler on my car. I swear it's about to fall off," Caroline stammered.

"Remind me when you come by the office," he uttered, narrowing his eyes.

"Good to meet you, Joy." She slowly walked

away from the table, but Rich could see the frown on her face.

After she had gone, Joy let out a deep breath and said, "Gee, talk about abrasive."

"I'm sorry. Don't let her get to you. She can be rude, I know. I've known her all my life. She sometimes shows other redeeming qualities, but they are only displayed occasionally." Rich leaned back and took a sip of water. He hadn't wanted to admit to Joy that in truth Caroline was a total snob. "I'm used to her because we grew up to-gether."

"How nice," Joy commented. Rich could tell she was not sincere when she said, "It's important to have friends from your youth." She took a long sip from her glass. Her fiery temper made her skin glow; he'd noticed it this afternoon.

He then cleared his throat and ran his hand through his hair. "Joy, do you like to dance at all?"

Her face lit up. "Of course I do. They're play-ing one of my favorites right now."

"Good, shall we?" He pushed back his chair, rose to his feet, and extended his hand to her. "I somehow knew you'd like this. You move so gracefully."

"Are you saying I'm the artsy type?" She laughed as she asked that question, and shook her gorgeous mane of red hair.

He pulled her close to him once they were on the dance floor. It was a slow song so he had a good excuse to be next to her. He liked the flowery soft scent of her skin.

"It's a perfect night for dancing," Joy said in his ear. "I can't think of a better way to spend the evening."

"Now we can really talk. Tell me what you did before you sold toys," he asked as he pulled her to him.

"Now, that's a good question," she answered, turning to look directly into his face. "Well, I went to art school many years ago and majored in animation, but I never got a job with a cartoon studio, so I worked a series of odd jobs . . . you know the story."

"No, I want to hear all about it from you," he said, turning his head to look at her face. "And what possessed you to start your shop?"

"Oh, I don't know. After years of going to hobby shows and reading countless books on toys and saving all my money, I just came to the conclusion I had to start this shop. I feel privileged to be able to make a living doing something I truly enjoy, but I don't lead a very luxurious life."

"Did you ever put your animation skills from school to any kind of use?" he asked, wrinkling his brow.

She laughed loudly, and he liked her gregarious

laugh. "I guess you could say I use my skills each day. But to answer you, yes, I did—I worked for a company that made greeting cards and drew cartoon characters for a while. I did mostly designs and slogans. Running a toy dealership is more fun."

"You call yourself a toy dealership, but that sounds like you're selling used cars or ripping people off." He laughed aloud.

"Well, enough about me. I really want to hear about you. Tell me all about yourself."

He paused and looked down at her smiling warm face. She was genuine. Should he tell her the truth? "To tell you the truth, I've never really loved insurance. I simply took over the family's share for my father after my wife left."

"My!" she gasped. "I'm sorry; I didn't realize." He saw that her cheeks were becoming very pink now.

"Are you shocked that I don't love insurance, or that I had a wife?" he asked, shaking his head. "As for my wife, you've nothing to feel sorry about, Joy. You had no idea I was ever married. It was a mistake. You know, I asked you here to talk about other things, but I'm glad you want to know more about me . . . that is the purpose of a first date."

"How long has it been, Rich, since the divorce?" She had stopped moving to the music and her face was only inches away from his. He could hear the sympathy in her voice.

"We broke up two years ago this summer," he said, looking away from her toward the window. "Margie left me to pursue her career. We didn't want the same things in life. Thank goodness, we realized it before we had kids. There's not much else to tell. At the end of the marriage, Margie wasn't the woman I had fallen in love with at all. She'd become obsessed with making it big." He knew he could not bear to tell her more than that; he'd told her too much already. One day he might be able to forget her and all the pain and suffering.

"Whatever happened, it sounds like you blame yourself, Rich." She paused as she looked into his eyes. How did she know that?

"Well, maybe I do; I don't know. Let's just say it was all very complicated. I don't want to ruin the evening by talking about it now." He knew he was keeping her at arm's length with his last statement. As they danced he held onto Joy tightly even though he was not sure he could trust her. Why? Could she make him forget the bitter marriage? A new feeling seemed to be awakening within him.

"I know how hard it can be to get over prior relationships. I've had one haunting me, but we were never even close to married. He's just someone I'd like to forget." She looked over his shoulder as she spoke, and he could tell she wanted to tell him more, but he wasn't sure he should hear more. This evening was moving too quickly.

"Let's go have some dinner, shall we?" he said as soon as the music stopped. "We can continue this conversation later."

"Sure," she said looking straight into his eyes. Her blue eyes reminded him of drowning pools. He felt lost in them, and he felt his heart start to beat faster.

Then it happened in a second. His eyelids lowered and his mouth quivered beneath his mustache as he felt his head come forward. His lips descended upon hers in a kiss. He felt her arms encircle his neck; she wasn't pulling away. Time was suspended as the warmth of her soft body seemed enveloped in his. From a distance, he heard a glass shatter on the floor. He and Joy pulled back from the shock of the sound at the same time.

Several heads in the room turned to look at the table from which the sound had come. Caroline was sitting at the table with her father. She pulled her chair away from the spot where the shattered glass lay. A waiter emerged from a side door with a dustpan and broom and began to sweep away the broken pieces. Rich could not look at Caroline right now, who he was certain was looking at the two of them.

"Let's go eat, Joy. I'm hungry."

"Sure, me too." She nodded. "However, I need to go to the ladies' room to freshen up."

Joy was certain that Caroline had meant to break that glass. What was going on between that woman and Rich? She reapplied her lipstick and wiped the sweat from her brow. That sure was some kiss. Why had it just happened? It was a mistake, and obviously he didn't seem to want to talk about it any more than she did, so it was best to let it go . . . wasn't it?

Just then the door opened and in walked Caroline. Joy immediately closed her bag and darted toward the door.

"Sure is one hot summer night," she said over her shoulder as she exited the bathroom.

Caroline only turned and glared at her.

Dinner was a very quiet affair. Neither of them had much to say. They were both struggling to be pleasant, and not a word was said about the kiss.

After he drove her home, Rich kissed her on the cheek and said, "Joy, I have to tell you, I can't remember when I've had such an enjoyable evening. We'll have to do this again soon."

"Thank you, I enjoyed myself too, but we never did get to discuss those trains that interested you so much this afternoon."

"No," he said, shuffling his feet. "But we'll have to do that someday soon, and we can also discuss other things then."

She simply laughed and watched him turn and walk down the stairs to go. After he left her apartment, she watched his car drive away from the window.

However, the spell was broken when she looked down to see a strange car parked at the curb. The driver appeared to be looking up at her apartment window. Then the engine of the car started, making a loud obnoxious roar as it slowly drove away.

Chapter Five

Joy unlocked the door to the shop and put the *Open* sign in the window. She peeked around the front door briefly to see if Cassie's flower shop was open yet. Darn, she wasn't there, and Joy was desperate to talk to someone about the events of last night. She was about to pick up the phone and call Cassie's home number when the bell over the shop door rang. Joy turned her head just in time to see Caroline walk into her store.

The sleek blond woman was dressed to perfection in a black silk business suit with a crisp white blouse underneath. Her blond hair just touched her shoulders. Although her lovely face wore no make-up, her piercing blue eyes screamed for a confrontation.

"Well, I must say, this is a cute little toy store," Caroline said as she walked around, looking in the toy cases.

"Is there something I can help you with, Caroline?" Joy asked firmly as she moved behind the cash register.

"I'm not here to buy any over-priced toys, if that's what you're wondering," Caroline snapped.

"No, I clearly get the impression you have something more pressing on your mind."

"Actually, I'm here about your little business meeting with Mr. Buckley last night. I do have to be—"

"Concerned?" Joy interrupted, finishing her sentence and raising an eyebrow.

Caroline leaned across the front counter so that her face was only a foot away from Joy's. Her tone changed dramatically to a husky whisper. "I have to be concerned as his lawyer. You know, Rich has gotten himself entangled in some nasty lawsuits. The particulars are ghastly, and I can't divulge details, so I won't go into it. I'm afraid I know him all too well, and you don't know a thing about him and his past."

Joy's mouth dropped two inches. She felt a shock wave sweep over her body. The feeling left her nauseated. "My goodness," was all she could whisper.

"Yes," Caroline continued, stepping back from

the counter. "You know, he and I were supposed to be married long ago, but then it never happened because he dumped me for Margie. I thought I should warn you about about what sort of man you're involved with here."

"I see," Joy replied softly as she swallowed hard.

"Yes, I'm glad you do see. He made a wreck of my life," Caroline said as she patted her hair. "Oh, I've gotten over it, but a gal like you should beware. He's a real headcase, sweetheart. You don't want to know about other things. I'm sure he probably told you all about Margie."

"He did tell me some," Joy answered, looking away from Caroline. She could not stand to look at the young woman's face twisted with anger.

"He's got real problems, and that Margie really screwed up his head." Caroline let out a laugh. "Imagine, after all I'd been through with him already. You have no idea how long I waited to set a date for the wedding, and now I'm his lawyer protecting him from himself most of the time. Fancy that, can you?"

Joy felt another shock wave. Was this guy really that much of a cad? What had he done to warrant lawsuits?

"You do understand why I came here then to talk to you, don't you? You must realize why I reacted the way I did to your intimacy with him out there on the club dance floor. He's now my client to worry about, and he's been so wracked up over Margie for so long he doesn't think straight, and he does dumb things. So I felt I had to follow you back last night and make sure nothing happened."

"You followed the car back here from the club?" Joy looked incredulously at the other woman. "I appreciate the warning, Ms. Voucher, as I had no idea such a situation existed, but all you had to do was come talk to me. You're right—I don't know him that well, and I should be more careful." She felt her heart sinking within her chest, and looked down at the floor to avoid having to look at the woman on the other side of the counter.

"He has this way with people, you know. I bet he even gave you the impression that his ex-wife was some villainess who caused him real pain, right?" Caroline's expression was sympathetic as she folded her arms across her chest.

Joy looked at her and nodded, but she felt very confused. Something in Caroline's voice was odd. There had to be more to the story, but she didn't know what to say. Last night *had* seemed too romantic to be real. Caroline had followed Rich's car to keep him out of trouble . . . wasn't that sort of behavior a bit extreme for a concerned lawyer?

Joy gazed at her dolls, so picture-perfect. Life

was never perfect, and humans far from it. Last night had only been an illusion. Had she really been nothing but the pawn of a man who was a skilled manipulator? He had kissed her tenderly right there in front of a large crowd of people and he had felt no embarrassment. He was probably used to overpowering people.

"Well, Caroline, I just don't know what to say. He didn't say much of anything about you and him."

"No, he wouldn't, I'm sure. He never does, and he'll never get over his ex-wife. He's been burned once and vowed not to let it happen again." Caroline shook her head and walked to the shop door. "I am warning you, though: stay away from him for your own good, lady. I'm sorry to have to come out here like this. Now, I'd better go."

Joy said nothing but nodded as Caroline left the shop.

She spent the afternoon straightening out the shelves of bears, and then called a local newspaper photographer to set up an appointment to photograph the two most valuable Ronnie dolls. She wanted to talk to Cassie and wondered why she hadn't heard from her friend yet. She really needed to confide in someone right now.

Finally at four o'clock Cassie walked into the shop. "What a day! Those wedding arrangements took all morning. I haven't had a day this busy in months!" Cassie put two cups of coffee on the counter top. Joy darted over to her friend and gave her a big hug.

"Cassie, I'm so glad to see you. You wouldn't believe all that's happened in the last twenty-four hours."

Joy immediately recounted all the details of her night at the country club and her morning conversation with Caroline. She left out no details. Cassie was all ears. She gasped when Joy told her about Caroline following them back to her apartment. Cassie began to ask a barrage of questions, mostly centered around Caroline Voucher.

"I don't know, Joy. I'd like to know more about this Caroline Voucher woman. She sounds very strange to me. Describe her again." Cassie slowly sipped her coffee.

"She's lovely, really. I mean she's petite, thin, blond and very aristocratic looking." Then Joy let out a sigh. "She looks like the type who never has to worry about her weight like I do."

"Joy Smathers, stop knocking yourself. Don't go comparing yourself with this woman. I don't like the sound of her, and you said Rich admitted she was obnoxious. However, it is strange that he's been friends with her for years," Cassie said, putting down her coffee cup.

"She's his partner's daughter, but I don't know

how to describe their relationship. She seems to want to have control over him in a weird way." Joy licked her lips after sipping the hazelnut coffee.

Just then the doorbell rang. "Delivery for Joy Smathers," called a uniformed man through the door.

Cassie and Joy looked at each other. Joy nodded to the man as she took the long white box from him. She laid it on the counter and opened it. She gasped when she saw the dozen red roses inside, and took out the small card.

Joy, Thank you so much for the loveliest evening of my entire life. You're a most wonderful and adorable woman.

Rich

"Wow, do you have any idea what it costs to send a dozen roses these days? These roses are locally grown, too, not frozen. They must have cost him a fortune." Cassie could not take her eyes off the box as she fingered the roses.

"Cass, don't be too impressed. This guy's got tons of money. I just don't know what to do now." She sighed and put her hands on her hips.

"I think you need to confront him about what Caroline has told you."

"No, I think it would probably be better if I just never saw him again. I'll just ignore him if he calls."

"How ridiculous can you be! You can't believe everything you hear, and he's going to call you again, and you need to be fair. Something's rotten in Applebloom Country Club here. Ask him all the questions that are burning in your mind right now. I don't trust this woman, Joy. She's telling you a tale for a reason."

Cassie drained her coffee cup and pushed back her short bobbed hair with a flick of her right hand. She shook her head emphatically.

"You really think she's lying, Cass?"

"A man just doesn't bring a woman to a country club where his ex-fiancée is dining. He's more careful than that. Something about her story doesn't make any sense."

"Well, I sure don't want to be his next victim," Joy snapped.

"Joy, you need to give him a chance to explain. Like I said, I smell a rat, and it may not be Rich." Cassie tossed her cup into a nearby trash can.

"She may be telling the absolute truth, Cass. After all, I hardly know this guy. Yet, he sends me a dozen roses after only one date. Sounds like a real charmer, I think."

"Joy Smathers, I know you well enough to

sense that you don't want to believe all she told you this morning either. And—"

"And what?"

"And I think a woman who follows her ex-fiancé's car back to another woman's apartment has some definite problems of her own," Cassie replied as she tapped her index finger on her forehead. "Now, moving onto other things, are you ready for the big doll show in the city next weekend?"

Rich Buckley walked down the street, grinning. He was thinking about the roses he'd sent Joy, and he didn't know why he felt so excited. It had been a tough day at the office, with lots of arguing with Joe Voucher. But he was approaching Joy Smathers' shop. Hopefully she'd be inside. When he approached the window, he could see she was sitting drinking coffee with her friend.

"Good afternoon, ladies. Joy, I see you got my flowers." Then he paused and added. "So it's coffee break time, eh."

He thought she looked stunning in a T-shirt and khaki slacks. Her unruly hair hung about her shoulders. He rubbed his thumb and forefinger over his mustache as he smiled at her.

"Mr. Buckley, you sure do know how to pick flowers. My husband always picks up roses that die in two days because they're frozen," Cassie said, leaning across the counter and turning her head to him.

"I'm amazed you can find time to take a coffee break, Cassie. I just passed your flower shop and noticed your shop's real busy. That young girl in there really has her hands full."

"Yes, I know, but I need my daily break. However, since you've made me feel so guilty, I guess I better get back. I don't want Stella to feel overwhelmed. Good to see you again, Mr. Buckley." Cassie then moved to the shop door to leave.

He watched Joy wave good-bye to her friend. He felt his stomach begin to twitter as soon as she left. Joy looked nervous too as she moved back toward the cash register and turned away from Rich.

"Joy, I really do want to know more about the train set, and—"

"Rich," she interrupted, turning her head to look at him, "I'm flattered by your attention, but I feel we need to talk."

"We sure do, lady. Let me come and get you tonight around seven. I know the perfect place to go for a nice quiet dinner." He paused and took a step closer to her, inhaling her flowery scent. "Then we can talk about all the other things you like in life other than toys." Something was happening to his senses.

"Oh, really?" she asked, not at all sure what to say.

"Yes, ma'am, and I think you should know I meant every word I wrote on that card." He smiled at her once again as he spoke.

"And to how many others have you delivered that line?" Joy snapped.

"Why, none that I can remember," he answered in surprise. Did she want to be with him as much as he wanted to be with her? "I told you before, that was quite an evening. I can't even remember when I last enjoyed myself so much. Also, I wanted to ask you something personal."

Joy did not wait for his question. "Before you continue, I think you should know that your dear friend Caroline came here this morning to see me."

What was Caroline doing here?

"Oh dear, I really must apologize for whatever she said to you," Rich said slowly. "I know how she acts, because she has nothing going on in her life. I can just imagine what she said. She's a bit obsessive and nosy, and I hope she didn't upset you, or I'll have a talk with her when I see her."

Joy looked puzzled. "Well, I was just going to ask you about some of the things she said to me today."

"Oh, what did she say about me exactly?" he asked curiously.

"Well," Joy said as she leaned back against the wall. "She made some very specific references about your past, and—"

"Did she now?" he interrupted with a laugh. What game was she playing with him? "Joy, do you know how much you've made me realize I need to re-think my life?"

He could see her face begin to perspire. "She also said—"

"She doesn't know what you've shown me, Joy Smathers. I need to play more and work less. I need to lose myself again like I did in my youth, just like you said the other day. You have no idea what spirit you've awakened in me." He would not let her finish her sentence because it was important he tell her how he could now remember some happiness from his past, and not just painful memories.

He moved to touch her cheek. Her skin was moist, warm and soft. Was this moving too fast for both of them? "Joy, you're so magnificent. I haven't felt this way in years."

His heart was beating too fast. He needed her like he'd never needed anyone else. What was happening?

She looked at him in confusion. "Rich," she said after a long pause, "Rich, whatever's happening, we have to talk."

Just then the bell over the shop door rang and

his head snapped around just in time to see an older woman entering her shop. "Excuse me," she said.

Rich immediately stepped away from Joy. He could not tell if she was angry or just overwhelmed. They had been standing so close and he'd wanted to kiss her again. He hadn't felt so touched by a woman in a long time. Fortunately, the older woman seemed too busy looking at the dolls in the display case to notice anything odd going on behind the counter.

"Looks like you have a customer, Joy," he said after clearing his throat. He smiled sheepishly at the elderly matron who had just noticed the two of them. The woman was looking at the two of them in bewilderment.

"Look, I'll be back at seven. Dress casually. But I must tell you this place is special."

"Well, I do have to see what—"

"No protestations, Joy. Just be ready. Then we'll have that talk." He quickly made his way to the shop door and waved good-bye. This moment was important. He hadn't felt this way in years.

"My, what a handsome man!" he heard the old woman exclaim. "You sure are one lucky woman."

He then heard Joy let out a nervous laugh. "Yes, well, what can I say. He's a real charmer."

Yes, he was determined to make her a lucky

woman. He had to tell her everything about his past, and how he had felt this afternoon.

But Joy just stood there, flushed with embarrassment from what had just happened. Was he trying to manipulate her? This guy sure knew how to screw up a woman's head. She would have to keep her distance from him tonight and be firm; she was not going to play this charade any longer. When was he planning on telling her the truth about Caroline? She could not believe that something was happening that had never happened before—that was too dangerous. She was going to give him a piece of her mind tonight. She just could not let herself get physically close to him—then she'd lose her head.

Chapter Six

Why did she always get involved with problematic men? She slammed the door to her closet shut as she changed her clothes. Couldn't she meet the right guy just once—even if it didn't turn into a perfect marriage like Cassie's?

She pulled the lightweight pantsuit over her body furiously. She let her long red hair hang about her shoulders and put on a dab of make-up.

"I have to tell him that I don't want to see him anymore. It's got to be final." She spoke to her own reflection in the mirror. "I won't play his fool. He won't sweet-talk me." But she remembered the look in his eyes this afternoon—he looked like he'd had a revelation.

Her cat looked up at her from the corner of the

bed where he lay. He meowed as if agreeing with her. Just then the doorbell rang.

Rich stood there humming as she opened the door. He was dressed in khaki pants and a white shirt. A tan sport coat was slung over his shoulder. She was about to say something, but he stopped her. His face was bright with excitement.

"I can't wait to show you this restaurant. You'll love it. It's in a gorgeous spot."

"That's fine, but I hope this place isn't very expensive," she flatly stated, hoping she'd made it clear she wanted no obligation to him.

"No, it isn't, and I know we have a lot to talk about, Joy. Can you guess where we're going tonight?" He stepped forward to hold the door for her.

"No, I hate guessing games," she snapped.

He was silent, obviously taken aback by her tone. "Okay, that's fine. I guess I'll have to tell you then. We're going down to the Tugboat Café. You know there's an old boat down on the river, and it's been converted into a restaurant."

"Yes, I know it," she quipped. "Listen, Rich. I'm not sure if dinner out is such a good idea. There's a lot that I have to say to you, and a restaurant can be a bad place for such things."

"Okay, then let's hang out here and order takeout." His voice was full of enthusiasm for the idea.

No, she felt she had to avoid that option at all costs after what had happened in the shop today and at the club last night. He grabbed her hand and pressed it to his lips. There was a look of mischief in his eyes. Why did he have to be so charming?

"Nope, nope. Let's go to the restaurant. That was the original plan." She moved through the front door of her apartment and turned around with keys in hand to lock the door.

"Good, because I think you'll like this place a lot. The chef's a friend of mine, and he's expecting us."

She wasn't sure if he was oblivious to her mood or just ignoring it. Perhaps he just didn't care.

Joy was silent on the drive down to the river. She knew she was probably going to tell him off during dinner. Enough was enough. It made her angry that someone was playing with her, but she'd agreed with Cassie that she should give him a chance to explain himself. Still, he probably wouldn't be able to defend himself. She just knew she was right.

The car pulled up in front of a lovely large tug boat. It was now a restaurant, and it looked extremely romantic. The evening sky's bright colors loomed in the background.

Joy continued to look at the boat with fixed fascination. "Who owns this old tugboat?"

"I do," he answered as he opened the passenger side door. "Dad saw this boat as a great investment years ago, and I inherited it from him. He made it into a café, and I just hired my friend to be the chef. Bill's a great cook—wait 'til you see what's on the menu."

"It's lovely," she said, gazing at it in amazement.

The boat was painted a lovely shade of gray and looked inviting with its small tables on deck. The river was calm and peaceful. Since it was the only vessel moored at the river bend, it looked very impressive.

"I'm glad you like it, my dear." He bowed with an exaggerated gesture. "May I have your arm, dearest lady, as we walk up the gangplank?"

Just then Joy thought of something. "Rich, did you notice that we were being followed last night?"

He stopped and turned to look directly at her. "No, why would we be followed?"

"Rich, I think we had better level with each other about some things. For starters, Caroline followed us last night, and she came into my shop in a state." She stopped walking for a moment and stood still, waiting to see his reaction.

His jaw dropped. "You can't be serious. Caroline's nuts, but not nuts enough to do something like that." He then cleared his throat and added,

"Look, let's go sit down. Then you can tell me everything."

Before she could say another word, he took her elbow and led her up the gangplank to the deck.

"Rich, I know Caroline followed us. She admitted it this morning. I didn't get a chance to tell you all that happened this morning during her visit."

Joy stopped once they had reached the deck.

He then motioned for her to have a seat. "Max, bring us some iced tea!" he shouted to a nearby waiter. He then sat down and turned to look at Joy.

"I can't believe that woman. Why didn't you say something earlier today when I came in?"

Joy's face was beginning to flush with anger. If he hadn't gone on a blue streak messing up her head, she could've told him. "Rich Buckley, I was trying to talk to you seriously this afternoon, but you acted like you couldn't care less about what I had to say!" She crossed her legs and sat back in her chair. Then she turned her head away from him.

"How can you say that?" he asked. "Listen Joy, I'm sick of Caroline and her antics. I do want to know what she said, but I don't see why her curiosity should upset you. I know she's a nutcase, but ignore her nosiness. I have to put up with her because she's my partner's daughter. I came here to spend the evening with you, not talk about Caroline Voucher. I'll deal with her later."

Joy burst out laughing. "Rich Buckley, you're a fool. You really expect me to just dismiss what your lawyer tells me about your legal problems and your personal problems? Who else have you taken advantage of recently?"

He slid his chair back dangerously close to the railing of the boat, almost knocking it over as he stood up.

"What in the world are you talking about, Joy? What lawsuit? Was she talking about the one with the heiress who accused our company of ripping her off? That was her father's doing, really. I can't believe the evening is turning out this way. I've been worrying all day about how to express myself to you, and here you are accusing me of something Caroline told you about to rip me to shreds. Did you ever consider my point of view at all?"

Joy stood and moved back against the railing of the boat. He took a step closer to her. His anger was frightening. She gripped the rail in back of her. Was Caroline confused?

"You're really something!" he exclaimed.

"*I'm* something! As if you haven't taken advantage of me over the course of the last two days," she shouted as she took another step backward. His arrogance annoyed her.

"If you call kissing taking advantage of you, I recall you enjoying it just fine!" he yelled, smacking his fist in the palm of his hand.

"Oh, you!" she screeched, and turned around to slap his face.

However, she swung too hard and missed. She hit the railing with a bang, lost her balance and fell over the railing and into the water.

"Joy!" Rich shouted. He tossed aside his sports jacket and jumped into the river. He gasped for breath with each stroke as he swam.

When he reached her and held her up in his arms, she was limp, but he had gotten to her just in time. There was a large bump on her head— she must have hit the side of the boat when she fell overboard. Several spectators were gazing over the side of the boat at Rich holding Joy in his arms as he waded ashore.

He gazed down at her lovely face and her mass of wet hair.

"What the heck were we arguing about, anyway?" he muttered.

Chapter Seven

Rich looked down at Joy as she lay wrapped in a thick blanket. He put her in the spare bedroom on the second floor. His head hurt and his mind drew a blank. He couldn't even remember what had started the argument in the first place.

He saw that she was starting to stir, and leaned forward to whisper in her ear. "Joy, how do you feel?"

He watched as she turned her head sideways to look at him. He was leaning against the closet door and holding a cup of tea in his hand.

"Joy, you're at my place. You took a bad fall. What do you need?"

She opened her eyes slowly and began to look

around the room. Rich followed her gaze. The room had a large king-sized bed and sleek, modern furniture. Joy put her hand to her head.

"I'm sure you have one mega-headache. Do you remember anything about the evening?" Rich took a step forward and sat down on the edge of the bed. Holding out the cup of tea to her, he motioned for her to take a sip before he set it on the nightstand. "That's a bad bruise on your head. Do you want some aspirin?" He touched the big purple mark on her head lightly.

"Yes, please, but tell me where I am and what happened." She put her hand on her forehead as she spoke.

"Joy, you're in the guestroom at my house. I brought you here. I also called Cassie Fisher and told her all about what happened. She's on her way."

"But, what happened?" Joy was still rubbing her forehead. "I just remember falling."

"Yeah, you took quite a spill backwards, and I jumped in after you." He paused then spoke again. "Here, let me get you some aspirin."

He left the room abruptly. It seemed obvious that she could not remember the argument. Did she even remember that they had been on a boat?

He entered the room again with the aspirin and a glass of water and offered them to her. He paused nervously and added, "Joy, I wrapped you in that blanket and brought you here because I didn't know what else to do. You were a mess."

"Thanks," she answered. "Is there a bathroom where I can freshen up?"

He wasn't sure she understood the full implication of what he had just said. He had wrapped her lovingly in that blanket and had cared about what happened to her. "I don't think you should try to walk by yourself just yet. The bathroom's at the end of the hall."

As he spoke, he put his arm around her waist and helped her to her feet. She leaned against him for support and he pulled her even closer to him. He walked with her from the large bedroom to the bathroom. Then she suddenly gasped.

"What is it, Joy?" Rich asked.

"I've never seen a chandelier that big," she said, pointing to the family heirloom which hung over the bannister in the hallway. She then gazed around the hallway at the Oriental rugs and wallpaper. "Your house is enormous."

At the end of the corridor they stopped. He opened the bathroom door and handed her Margie's old sweatsuit. "Cassie should be here soon. I made some broth; I'll bring some to you. Why don't you change?"

"Rich, does Cassie know how to get here?" she asked, rubbing her temples.

"Yes, I gave her directions. Is your head still hurting?" He gripped her waist tighter.

"How did you get Cassie's number?"

"There are only two Fishers listed locally. I figured I had to tell *someone* where you were, and I didn't know anyone in your family. I'm sorry about bringing you back here, but you were soaked, and you seemed shocked by what happened."

She looked at him with a dazed expression on her face. "I feel much too awful to care right now. I know we had some harsh words, but I don't even remember what they were about. And I am glad you called Cassie instead of my mother—thank heaven you don't know *her* phone number. Do you remember what we argued about?"

"Look, we'll talk about it all later. Now's not the time to discuss anything intense, okay?"

When he came back upstairs, he saw she was lying back down on the bed with her right hand on her forehead. He set the tray of broth on a table near the bed and then sat down next to her. He reached over and patted her hand.

"Look, I was really worried. Your fall really scared me." He wasn't sure what he should say next. Should he tell her that Caroline was simply desperate for a husband, and for some reason she wanted him? Or would that strike Joy as arrogant?

"Ugh, thank goodness it's over. I'm sure I'll be

fine by tomorrow morning." She sat up again and pushed back the pillows on the bed. "I *have* to be fine by tomorrow."

"Have to be?" he asked.

"There's a photographer coming to photograph Mrs. Michaels's Ronnie dolls tomorrow, and I hope to get good publicity for them since the doll show's coming up. It'll be my biggest chance this year. I owe it to Loretta Michaels."

"Are you sure you're up to it?" Rich asked, raising an eyebrow. "Your loyalty to her goes beyond the grave, doesn't it?"

"Well, this business is my life now. It's become more to me than just my livelihood. I've gathered that your business is the center of your life, too. But to answer your question, yes, Mrs. Michaels was a dear friend as well as my backer. I cared about her very much."

"Well, I know you argue as passionately as you work, which leads me to what I must say." He licked his lips. "I have a feeling Caroline told you some pretty big lies about me." He leaned closer to her as he spoke, but just then the doorbell rang. He jumped up from the bed. "Excuse me, I'd better get that. It's probably Cassie."

He raced down the stairs quickly and opened the door, only to see Caroline standing there with a worried look on her face.

"Caroline, what are you doing here?" he asked, trying to control his anger.

"Rich, something's happened," she said, walking through the doorway with tears in her eyes.

"Caroline, I need to know everything you've been saying about me. Joy's told me some things."

"Rich," she put a hand up to cover his mouth, completely ignoring what he'd just said, "something terrible's happened. Dad's had a heart attack. He's been talking about you, and I've been too confused and upset to know what to do. You've got to come, Rich." Caroline took a handkerchief out of her shirt pocket and began to wipe her eyes.

"I'm sorry, Caroline. How bad is it?" He took a step away from the door. *Why does this have to happen now?*

"Very bad, Rich. I think Dad needs to talk to you. He's at Devon Lane Hospital." She blew her nose into the handkerchief. "You know he's always considered you a son, not just a partner. Your father and he were so close."

"Well, Caroline, I can't go right now. Joy's had a terrible accident. I need to help her right now."

Caroline's face turned a bright fiery red. Then she swallowed slowly. "Is Joy here right now?"

"Yes, she's in the blue guest room. Now, why

don't you go down to the hospital, and I'll come later. I promise."

"Hello," said a voice from behind Caroline. "I'm glad I finally found your place." Cassie moved through the doorway, gazing at Caroline with interest. Cassie then turned her head slightly to look at him. "Sorry way to start a date, huh?" she said to Rich as she brushed past him.

"Cassie, I'm glad you're here. Joy's upstairs." Cassie winked at him. As she climbed the stairs, he noticed she still watched Caroline, who was blowing her nose and wiping her eyes.

Joy was trying to listen in on the conversation downstairs when she heard Cassie's voice. She remembered now that Caroline's allegations had been the source of their argument. A few seconds later, she looked up to see Cassie standing in the doorway.

"Joy, are you okay? I heard all about your accident. That's a nasty mark on your forehead there. But tell me, what happened?"

"Cassie," Joy whispered loudly as she sat up and moved closer to the edge of the bed, "what's going on downstairs?"

Cassie moved closer to the bed and then kneeled down next to it so she could face Joy at eye level. "That little whip Caroline is downstairs. Do you know she's been browsing in my flower shop several times over the last couple of days? What a mean looking woman!"

Joy set aside the tray Rich had brought for her. "I'm ready to go. I can talk to Mr. Buckley another time. I do have to get up early since the newspaper photographer's coming tomorrow, and I need time to think."

She got up from the bed and rubbed her eyes. Just then she heard Rich's voice in the hallway.

"Caroline, I have to see how Joy is. I said I'd meet you at the hospital in a half-hour."

"Rich, you have to realize how important it is for you to come. I'm so worried about him." Caroline's voice was cracking.

Then the front door closed.

They heard footsteps approaching. Joy and Cassie just looked at each other silently. A few seconds later the knob on the bedroom door turned. Rich came in looking puzzled.

"Well, Joy, will you take a rain check?" She burst out laughing, and he smiled, but then looked down at the floor as he said, "I realize this is not the best way to end the evening, but I think you should go home and rest. And I need to go to the hospital—my partner appears to be seriously ill."

Joy stood up slowly, holding onto Cassie's arm for support. "Thanks, Rich. I understand you need to go. I also need to be getting back."

"I can't believe you're going to set up those dolls tonight," Cassie said incredulously.

"I'll stop by and see you tomorrow then." He moved away from the bedroom door so she could pass him.

Joy stopped and looked at him. "Rich, I'll be busy, but we'll have another time."

He swallowed. "Yeah, I know. You've accused me of being a workaholic, but you're the one who's talking about how busy you are with your work."

Before she could answer, Cassie exclaimed, "You're so thoughtful, Rich. You and Joy can have that little talk you need to have then."

Joy turned her head quickly to glare at her friend, and said "I need to get home."

She was too confused to say anything more.

"I hope you locked up the shop downstairs," Cassie said as Joy unlocked her apartment door. "Mrs. Myers told me there's been a few burglaries in the neighborhood recently."

"Cassie, Mrs. Myers likes to talk. Right now I need to set up those dolls, and then call it a night. I need to lie down."

"Well, before you go lie down, exactly how did you fall overboard at that restaurant tonight? Rich only gave me some sketchy details." Cassie moved to Joy's sofa and plopped herself down on it.

"Oh, I don't know what to say, Cass. One minute I was screaming at him, then I stepped back and fell. I don't remember what he said, either. Next thing I know I awoke in wet clothes in his guestroom."

"You were *screaming* at him?" Cassie wailed, slapping her forehead. "Can't you ever hold your temper? So you didn't even give him a chance to defend himself, after all I told you before you left?"

"Cassie, I'm going to get the dolls to display on the kitchenette table for the photo. I'm not discussing Rich again with you tonight. Now, you said you'd help me, so please do so I can go lie down."

"Relax, Joy, some collector will see those dolls in the paper and be eager to buy. The Cancer Foundation will get its donation and your shop will continue to gain customers. I think your personal life needs attention right now. Your friend Rich has problems you should find out more about."

Joy shook her head and walked slowly down the stairs to the shop. Rich Buckley was too overwhelming to think about right now.

Her friend followed her, continuing her monologue. "That man scares you, Joy."

Joy rolled her eyes. "Cass, cool it."

"Joy, did you hear that!" Cassie suddenly exclaimed in a loud whisper.

As Joy turned to look at her, Cassie put a finger to her lips. "Shh,"

"What is it, Cass?"

"I heard something downstairs in the shop. Didn't you?"

"No," Joy answered, pausing for a moment before opening the back door to the shop. "Cassie, please don't scare me like that."

"I am not trying to scare you. I heard something."

"Well, I didn't." Was Rich on her mind too much lately?

"Look," Cassie gasped, pointing to a pile of bears on the floor as Joy opened the door.

"Cassie, please calm down," Joy said as she turned on the light and moved toward the safe.

She looked around the room quickly and then opened the safe. Fortunately both the 1962 Ronnies were there in their original boxes. However, the padlock to the safe was upside down. Had it been that way before she left? She *had* left the shop in a hurry.

"Does anything seem out of the ordinary to you?" Cassie asked.

Joy quickly moved about the room. Nothing seemed to be missing, but the teddy bears on the floor were a strange sight. There was no breeze to have knocked them over.

"Everything's here from what I can see."

"I was just thinking—"

"Cassie, enough, okay? You've just about given me a heart attack. They probably just fell over," Joy said, tucking the dolls under her arm. "Let's go set these dolls up for display. Would you grab some of the other Ronnies on the shelf?"

Cassie took two more old Ronnie dolls from the display case and followed Joy back up the stairs. "You do like him, Joy, don't you? You're just feeling disappointed about him."

"Cassie, you're beginning to sound like my mother."

"Okay, well when's this woman coming over to photograph the dolls?" Cassie asked, setting them down on the kitchenette dining table.

"Anyway we come from different sides of the track, Cass. It's not looking good. What that woman told me about him may not be true, but I'm not sure it really matters. I don't know if I should get involved with him."

Cassie giggled and said, "You'd better take the sweatsuit back to him."

"Right. I'll go to his office tomorrow before I open the shop and take it back to him." She knew she was saying this out loud for a reason. "Why do you suppose he has a woman's jogging suit at his place?"

"Probably his ex-wife's," Cassie said immediately.

Chapter Eight

"Mr. Voucher will be fine. He'll be able to go home after a couple of hours of observation," the nurse said to Caroline, sitting on the lobby couch.

Rich shifted his feet and stuck his hands in his pockets. He wanted to cuss Caroline out for dragging him down to the hospital for this false emergency.

"But it *could've* been a heart attack, right?" Caroline said to the nurse. "I mean, Daddy was all sweaty and I thought for sure—"

"Well, he'll be fine, miss. I think he just had a dizzy spell in this heat. But we are checking everything out just to make sure. You know that extreme heat affects the elderly the most."

The nurse then turned to go down the hospital corridor. Rich could not bear to look at Caroline.

"I was just so worried," Caroline wailed, chewing on her lower lip.

Rich simply looked out the hospital window as he said, "Caroline, I think I'll be going now. It appears that everything is—"

"Oh no, Rich," she interrupted. "Please don't leave me here all alone. All of this has scared me."

"Your father's going to be fine," Rich muttered, still gazing out the window.

"Rich, he was asking for you. You know he thinks the world of you. When your father and he were partners—"

"Caroline," he snapped, "I don't have time for games. You shouldn't have dragged me down here until you knew for sure it was serious. I think a lot of your father, too, but his health isn't in any grave danger, and I don't appreciate you giving me a scare like this." He rubbed his eyes with his thumb and forefinger. "You also interrupted my evening."

"Well, I thought you would be at the office working late. . . . you can imagine my shock."

"Caroline, what did you say to Joy? You obviously gave her a bad impression of me. She thinks I'm some sort of insensitive jerk."

"Rich, what makes you think I said anything

false?" Caroline smiled sweetly at him as she spoke.

"Caroline, I've known you too long."

"Richard Buckley, I can't believe you don't realize by now that the only thing I want is your happiness. I'm your oldest friend, remember. Just what did Joy say?"

"Somehow you gave her the idea that I'm a real heartless businessman who's got a quirky hang up with women," he said, shaking his head. "You know I haven't had a social life since Margie left."

"Rich," Caroline said, crossing her arms. "I think she probably misunderstood what I said."

"You also gave her the impression somehow that the two of us were seriously involved," he said, knitting his eyebrows together.

Caroline let out a nervous laugh. "You know how we used to joke and play around when we were kids, saying we'd be married one day." Caroline laughed again. "She probably didn't realize I was just kidding around when I said those things in her shop that day."

"Mm-hm," Rich muttered. "Take you father home and tell *him* to call me if he needs me. I've got to go." He knew he could not mask his disgust with her anymore.

"Rich, I never meant to cause any problems, but aren't you going to see Daddy before I take him home?"

"No, tell your father I'm glad he's okay, but I've had a rough night. See you later."

Rich took a sip of his morning coffee and then rose to his feet. His secretary had said a woman was waiting for him in the office lobby. Hopefully, it wouldn't be Caroline.

Rich opened the door and saw Joy sitting on the lobby sofa with Margie's old sweatsuit under her arm. She was dressed up in a black and white silk dress, and her hair was piled on top of her head.

"I didn't expect to see *you* here today," he said, motioning for her to come into his office.

She smiled at him sheepishly and said, "I thought I'd better bring back this sweatsuit you lent me the other night. And I thought I should personally thank you for helping me, after—"

"Don't mention it," he interjected. "You do look lovely today." He only gazed at her, feeling the corners of his mouth twitch nervously.

"Oh well, my photo's going to be taken today since I'm displaying the Ronnie dolls for the local paper. I thought I should try to look my best."

"You do, and I'm glad you came here today. I felt bad about our evening not working out." He slid into the chair behind his cherry desk and nodded for her to sit down on a nearby loveseat.

"Well, I don't remember too much of what hap-

pened or why I got so angry before I fell overboard and hit my head." She scratched her
forehead and then added, "I'm sorry it didn't work
out too. By the way, how's your partner?"

"Oh, he's fine. It was just some sort of dizzy
spell, nothing serious." Rich paused. "You made
me feel terrible. I mean, Joy, I'm out of practice
here. You must believe me when I say I haven't
been with another woman since Margie walked
out. I'm sure you were misinformed about me and
that client—*she's* the one that made the fraudulent
accusations after we refused to pay her claim for
a phony fire."

"I see," Joy replied, looking down at the floor.
"Caroline didn't mention that. I should've been
more calm when I asked those questions. I think
her unexpected visit to the shop and all the stress
over the upcoming doll show made me lose my
cool in a way I shouldn't have."

He chuckled and then folded his hands on top
of the desk. "I am curious though, Joy. I mean
I'm divorced, and you know about me. But the
other night, you mentioned some guy you had
been serious about. Why didn't you marry him?"

"He left me for someone else. But why did—"
she paused.

"Yes?" he asked. "What is it?"

"Well, it was very hard for me when he left."
She was twisting her hands and turning away from

him as she rubbed her upper arms. "I thought we had a strong relationship." He watched her as she gazed down at the floor again. "But I was wondering if there were other reasons why your marriage didn't work out."

He let out a deep breath. "Remember I said we wanted different things?" He paused before adding, "I wanted children, but she didn't. I never realized we had such differences until I started talking about starting a family."

"Yes, well, we don't know what people are really like until we've lived with them for awhile."

Joy stood up and began to move toward the door. He could tell she was uneasy.

"You know, I really wish I'd met someone like you years ago," he said, rising from his chair. She stopped in her tracks and looked back at him over her shoulder. He then walked over to her and put a hand on her shoulder.

She laughed. "Well, who knows. Lots of things in life are a matter of timing. You said something yesterday about how I made you come to some realization."

"Right," he said in a low voice. "Looking at those trains made me remember happier times in my youth. I needed to remember happier times; I've been feeling numb for *years*, Joy. You know the night we first went out, it felt as if I'd known you forever. I felt so comfortable. I had to keep reminding myself that I'd only met you last week."

"Sounds like some sort of déjà-vu," she whispered. "I think you and I can both understand each other's interests. We both have a strong desire to recapture our childhoods."

"Oh?" he asked, raising an eyebrow. "Just exactly what do you mean?"

"I think there's a side of you that's more honest, carefree, and playful than you ever let on inside this office."

He laughed again. "You know, I think I now know why I am attracted to you so much. I like your candor."

"Well, I only believe in lying to protect someone's feelings. You understand that, don't you?" she asked, smiling at him. Her face was only inches from his.

"Yes, of course I do." He felt frozen gazing into her eyes. He wanted to lean forward and kiss her again just like he had the other night at the club. Now was the perfect moment.

Just then there was a knock at the door, and Rich jumped back.

"Yes," he called out. "I'm in a meeting. What is it?"

"Mr. Buckley, sir," a male voice said through the door, "there's a client here demanding to see you right now."

Joy simply smiled at him and raised an eyebrow. "I think it's time for me to leave."

She turned to go, but he grabbed her wrist and pulled her back toward him.

"Please let us continue this. I want to see you as soon as possible. How about tonight?"

"Well, you could—"

"Joy, I can't tell you how much I want to talk," he interrupted, trying to control the plea in his voice.

"Okay, give me a call later. But now I need to go and open up the shop."

He watched her walk out the door. Both James Pyle and his secretary were in the outer office area. They looked surprised when she stepped out of his office, but he didn't care what they were thinking.

Chapter Nine

She listened to the photographer's idle chatter as she sipped her coffee. The Ronnie dolls were set up on top of the shop counter. She went over and re-positioned one of the two 1962 Ronnies so that the $8,000.00 price tag showed.

"I can't tell you how much I loved my first Ronnie doll," the photographer said as she snapped a photo. "I bet you have a blast running a shop like this." The young woman from the newspaper with the thick glasses looked around the store. "I mean, this place is so cool. The reason I thought it would be best to photograph the dolls here is so that people can see your store in the background. You've got so many interesting pieces here."

Joy just smiled and nodded. Normally she would have enjoyed conversation with this interested young woman; she was so bright and bubbly. However, right now she was preoccupied with thoughts of Rich. The meeting in his office had really scared her for some reason. She'd just learned that he loved and wanted children as much as she did. Now she could not get his handsome face out of her head. Had she ever felt this way about Larson in the early days of their relationship?

Why had she felt so overwhelmed this morning? She was a grown woman. There was no reason for her to feel so in over her head. But had Larson ever confessed true feelings to her the way Rich had this morning? A jittery sensation had come over her when he'd started talking abut Margie, and she was certain he was telling the truth about what Caroline had said. . . . or did she just desperately want to believe him?

Why did these feelings seem so odd to her? When he'd said he wanted to see her later, did that mean he felt as connected to her as she felt to him? She knew he'd wanted to kiss her, and would have if they hadn't been interrupted, and her heart pounded heavily knowing that she gladly would have let him.

The newspaper photographer jerked her back to the present when she asked, "Ms. Smathers, can you stand next to the counter for the next picture?"

"Oh yes," she replied, shaking her head. "I'm sorry. I was so deep in thought I really didn't hear what you said."

"I bet it's nerve-wracking running a shop like this, with all these expensive little things. So many of them are breakable, too."

"Yes," Joy replied.

Just then the bell over the shop door rang, and Joy turned her head and almost gasped when she saw who was entering the store. It was Janet Swing, a well known dollar dealer. Her teased black hair reaked of cheap hairspray, and her rhinestone studded glasses were held between the long red nails of her thumb and forefinger as she walked into the shop.

"Hello, Janet," she said, trying to hide her contempt for the woman. Janet loved to exaggerate the value of the dolls she sold. She was known to re-package dolls and say they had never been removed from the box.

The photographer snapped another photo and then stepped away from the counter to reload her camera as Janet took a step closer. She put on her rhinestone glasses and leered at the two 1962 Ronnie dolls. Joy thought she would gag from the overwhelming odor of her cheap perfume.

"Well, I see you have the most coveted dolls in

America on display here. I've never seen a 1962 first edition blond Ronnie doll side by side with a brunet one. I hope those beauties bring in the pretty penny promised."

Joy just took a sip from her coffee mug and nodded. "Yeah, well, I hope to sell them soon, but I'm really not negotiable on the price."

"Didn't I hear that these dolls were part of someone's estate?" Janet asked, leaning closer to examine the two oldest Ronnies.

Joy leaned back against the wall. "Yeah, and the proceeds from the sale are going to the Cancer Foundation."

"Well, they certainly are a hot item, if they're the real thing. Tell me the truth from one dealer to another. Did you re-box them or do any re-painting? How about the hair? Is it the real thing?" Janet was leaning over the counter and her overly made-up face was only inches away from Joy's.

"No, Janet, they're real. I don't think it pays to misrepresent things."

Janet shrugged her shoulders and glanced around the shop. "Well, I hope you're getting some decent publicity with these dolls. I mean, I heard the collector who owned them was pretty eccentric and had an untimely death. But, my, those dolls really are in mint condition, aren't they. I'm sure their investment potential is great, too."

Joy just shook her head and bit her lower lip. "Only a very serious collector is going to want one and be willing to pay top dollar."

"Well, that doll is always going up in price, isn't she?" After looking at the dolls again, she turned her head. "But tell me, how's business, Joy?"

"Oh, pretty good right now."

"Uh-huh. Well, I did come here to check out these beauties for a reason," Janet said, turning to look directly at her. "I think these dolls are lovely, but hard-looking."

Joy snickered. She had always thought that Janet was very 'hard-looking'. "Well, Janet, as you know, make-up and hairstyles were different back in 1962."

Janet removed her glasses. "Just what makes you think I was around in 1962?" she asked with a snap.

"Well, since you know so much about dolls, I just figured—"

"Never mind," she interrupted. "What I want to know is, if I send a wealthy interested collector your way and she buys these dolls, will you give me a finder's fee?"

"Say, I think I'd better be going," the photographer interjected. "I've got a lot of work to do back at the paper." She was packing up her camera equipment as she spoke.

"Great," Joy said and turned to wave good-bye to the young woman. She was grateful for a distraction from Janet's offer.

"Oh, and the pictures should be in tomorrow morning's paper," the girl called back over her shoulder as she walked out the door.

Joy then turned her attention back to Janet Swing. "Well, Janet, I don't know. I wasn't planning to keep any portion of the money from the sale of these Ronnies. Mrs. Michaels specified in her will that she wanted all money from the sale of her most valuable dolls to go to cancer research. Those two Ronnie dolls are definitely two of her most valuable."

"A sixteen thousand dollar sale should earn me at least a five hundred dollar commission," Janet quipped in a nasty tone. "I don't know how many wealthy customers you have that can afford to pay such high prices around here. However, I know someone in Maryland who is willing to drive all the way up here to take a good look at these, and I think she'd buy."

Joy chewed on her lower lip. If she didn't take Janet up on her offer, she might not sell the two dolls. She had to decide quickly even though she didn't like Janet. "Okay, Janet, I'll see you get five hundred dollars if you send me a collector who buys both."

"Done deal," Janet said, extending a hand to

Joy. "And I expect you to refer some business my way in the future," she added, pointing a long finger in the air.

Joy shook her head as she watched the woman leave. Had she done the right thing? Janet had such a bad reputation. But why would she lie about a potential customer for a couple of eight thousand dollar Ronnies?

Well, if she had to give her a fee for sending a customer like that, it would be worth it. The Foundation would still get a sizeable donation from the sale.

Besides, she had more important things to worry about right now. What did Rich Buckley really want from her?

Two hours later a tall, gray-haired woman with a big hairdo and a Gucci handbag walked into the shop. She removed her sunglasses as soon as she saw Joy. "Ms. Smathers, I understand you're selling two original 1962 Ronnie dolls? I'd like to see them, please."

Joy jumped to her feet. "Sure, but you understand I can't really let you handle them too much. I can let you look at the dolls up close, but if boxes get marked or mishandled, that brings down the value of the doll."

"Of course, I understand." The woman nodded her head as she spoke.

Joy unlocked the case and held out the brunette Ronnie for the woman to see. The woman moved closer and peered at the doll in the box through a diamond-studded magnifying glass.

"Now, may I see the blond one as well?" she asked after a pause.

Joy smiled as she put the dark-haired Ronnie back into the case and then took out the blond. She could just feel the sale at the tips of her fingers.

"I'm impressed. They're in perfect condition. I suppose you'll want a cashier's check for such a large sale." The woman then folded the magnifying glass as she spoke.

"Yes, ma'am. If it was any other doll for sale or at a smaller price, like fifty dollars or less, then I could take a regular check, but unfortunately not in this case," Joy replied, locking the case.

"Well, I'm extremely interested. Could you hold them for twenty-four hours? I'm going to run over to my bank today. My trust officer can draw up a cashier's check immediately."

Joy clapped her hands together and then cleared her throat. "Which one of the two are you interested in Ms.—?"

"Meg Hamilton," the woman answered with a wave of her hand. "I want both of them, dear."

"Really?" Joy let out a gasp. "Well, I'll certainly keep an eye on them until you get back.

I'm sure nobody's going to come in to buy these two dolls in the next twenty-four hours."

"You must tell me what the sale tax is, of course."

Joy took out her calculator. She could feel her hands shaking and tried her best to chat pleasantly. She thought how pleased Loretta Michaels would have been to sell the dolls so quickly. She also realized she needed to call the paper right away and tell them that the dolls were sold.

Meg Hamilton chattered away about her collection. As Joy glanced out the window, her head jerked forward as she saw Caroline Voucher coming out of Cassie's flower shop with a bunch of gladiolas in her arms. She walked right past Joy's shop but didn't look in the window at all.

"Now, you've got to promise me that you're going to make sure nothing happens to these dolls before tomorrow," the woman said, wagging her finger at Joy. "I've been looking for years, and now I'm finally going to own the desired prize for all doll collectors. Janet Swing told the truth about them."

"Ms. Hamilton, I'll be looking forward to your return tomorrow, and have a safe trip back home. You're making a wonderful acquisition for your collection."

Chapter Ten

"Gee, you mean you actually may have sold those outrageously priced Ronnie dolls?" Rich asked, laughing. "Maybe that'll make up for your tumble from the boat last night."

"I still have a headache from that fall, but I'm feeling better now," Joy said with a chuckle.

Rich leaned over the shop counter. "Joy, I came down early to ask you to go on a picnic with me. Close the shop and come with me. It's a perfect day to spend in the park," he said, reaching over to touch her hand.

Joy smiled, but he could tell she was hesitant. She looked like she needed some fun right now. "Well, I don't know if I should, Rich. It's still early afternoon."

"And you say *I'm* single-minded about work. Here I took the entire afternoon off so I could come here and see you, and you feel the need to keep working."

"But it's more than two hours 'til closing," she said, looking at the clock.

"Look," he said gently stroking her hand. "Call it an early day. Let's go celebrate the big sale. I've got a basket of sandwiches in the back of the car. Please, let's go."

"Okay, you've made it too tempting," she said with excitement. He watched as she hung a *Closed* sign in the window. "Now, let's go."

An hour later they were sitting under a tree on a patch of grass eating sandwiches.

"Joy, here's to you and your marvelous sale," he said, raising a plastic cup in the air.

"Thanks," she said giddily. "You know, it's beautiful out here. I do need to take the rest of the day off." She took another sip of soda. "So, do you come here often?"

"I used to when I was a boy," he said with a frown. "Mother used to send me here with the nanny for the day."

"So you came here with your nanny when you weren't playing with your toy trains?"

"Yes," he answered, leaning back against the tree. "But I preferred playing inside with my toy train sets most of the time."

"And what did you play?" she asked eagerly, grinning at him.

He looked up at the sky and swallowed. Should he tell her the sad games he'd made up as a child?

"Well, for starters, I used to pretend there was a town where everything was bad, but once the train came through, things changed dramatically for the better. On days when I was sad, like when my mother died, I played that the train was evil and it was passing through the town and making everything in the perfect little town bad. Now that I look back on it, my games mirrored my feelings."

"Rich," Joy said softly, "you've suffered a lot in your life."

"I've always felt that sometimes evil charges through our lives like a speeding freight train. I loved my mom so much, but she died when I was young. I think I may have married Margie because she looked and acted a lot like her."

"I see," she said in a hoarse whisper. "It sounds like you were very troubled by some things in your youth."

"Yes, I can remember that I was," he said sadly, shaking his head. Then he turned to face her. "I can also remember feeling that way when Margie and I broke up. It felt like something horribly uncontrollable had steamrolled its way into our lives and ruined all we'd had."

"Well, I can relate to that feeling. I felt helpless to understand why Larson and I could not be together."

Rich stared straight ahead, deep in thought. They shared so many feelings in common, and she knew how he felt. However, he feared this hour of revelation, and told himself to change the subject.

"Rich?" she asked as she picked a blade of grass with her finger tips, "just what is going on with Caroline?"

"Ha!" he exclaimed with a chuckle. "As if I know. Whatever it is, I don't want to discuss her now."

"But why did she say her father had a heart attack?"

"So you heard about that," he said, shaking his head. "Well, he had a spell, and I went to go see him. I don't know if she was really scared or just wanted attention."

Rich was silent and leaned closer to Joy. She looked up at him and said, "I take it your relationship with her father is important to you, or you wouldn't have been so eager to leave last night."

"He was my father's business partner," he said, looking down at his feet. "But I'm not sure our business relationship is good." He clenched his teeth in disgust. "He wants to do things I just can't see doing."

"Such as?" she asked, raising an eyebrow.

"Well, he wants to expand the business to a ridiculous degree. My father was always content to focus on small to medium-sized businesses." He leaned back against the tree and rubbed his mustache. "I just don't need to own a million dollar company in my lifetime."

She threw back her head and laughed. "That sounds funny coming from a guy like you. Maybe we've got more in common than it appears."

It was dark when he dropped her off on Main Street, so she entered through the storefront. As she walked to the shop door, she thought about what a perfect gentleman he had been this afternoon. But she had wanted him to kiss her, and she wondered why he hadn't. He seemed troubled by the past and his life had been filled with so much pain. Hers had been too, but she wasn't as overly cautious as he was.

She noticed Cassie's shop was locked up tight. However, when she reached the front door of her store, she knew immediately that something was wrong. The window below the *Closed* sign had been smashed, and the door was ajar. She felt a wave of panic sweep over her body, and a sick feeling rose in her throat.

Joy slowly pushed the door open and began to look around, fumbling for a light switch. She gasped when she saw the huge hole in the front display case—the glass had been smashed and the two 1962 Ronnies were gone. The other dolls in the display case hadn't been touched.

She let out a wail and put a hand to her mouth when she remembered she hadn't put the dolls in the vault before leaving. How could she have been so careless?

Joy walked around the shop, frantically trying to figure out if anything else was missing. Nothing else seemed out of place. She put her hands over her eyes and tried to think. Her mind was in a fog, and she wanted to scream.

She slowly moved to the phone and called the police. "My shop's been burglarized," she said in a trembling voice.

She bit her lower lip to try to keep from crying as she gave the police her name and address. After they assured her someone would be coming over immediately, Joy hung up the phone and dialed Cassie's home number.

Chapter Eleven

"Joy, you need to sit down and relax," Cassie said, pulling up a chair for her. Joy sat down while the heavyset police officer looked around the store and made some notes. "I just have a feeling that those dolls haven't gone very far." Cassie reached over and patted her forearm.

"I just can't believe it," Joy said, staring down at the floor and shaking her head. "I even have a buyer who's supposed to be coming back tomorrow."

"What time did this potential buyer come in, ma'am?" the policeman asked, turning around to face her.

"I just don't remember. This woman came in, wanted to buy both of them, and said she was

104

getting a cashier's check from her bank. Those two Ronnies cost eight thousand dollars each." Joy held her head in her hands and sighed.

The policeman let out a low whistle. "And you say that's all that's missing here. Someone was actually willing to pay sixteen thousand dollars for two Ronnie dolls." The expression on the officer's face was incredulous.

"Sir, the toys my friend sells are genuine antiques. This is not a regular toy store here," Cassie interjected, still kneeling beside Joy.

"So let me get this straight. You left the shop, and when you got back you noticed it had been broken into." The policeman scratched his ear.

"I was in my shop next door all afternoon, and I didn't see anything strange." Cassie looked from Joy to the officer as she spoke.

Joy nodded but could not look at anyone. Everything that had happened today had been so unreal. She had returned feeling happy tonight, happier than she had felt in years, but the day had been sort of strange, as well. First, Janet Swing had come in curious about the dolls, and then an extraordinarily wealthy woman had showed up, wanting to buy both of them, but couldn't do it until tomorrow.

"You know, your alarm system has been tampered with," the policeman said. "I'm wondering if this was a real professional theft." Then he let out another whistle. "I don't know what's more incredible: the fact someone would pay sixteen thousand dollars for two dolls, or the fact that someone went to a lot of trouble just to steal them, and nothing else."

Joy could not look at the man, but she saw from the corner of her eye that Cassie was glaring at him. "Gee, I love your sense of humor, Officer," Cassie quipped. "And you know, there are lots of people who can deactivate security systems who aren't professional criminals."

A few seconds later, she turned her head when she heard the shop door bell sound. Rich was out of breath as he jogged through the front door.

"I called him," Cassie whispered in her ear, "right after you called me."

"Honey, I know you're in a state, but don't despair yet. We'll find those dolls," he said, kneading her shoulder. "Remember, I own the company that insures your dolls, and you won't be out a cent. I promise."

"It's not just the theft. I should've been more careful," Joy wailed. "I forgot to lock them up before we left this afternoon." She leaned back in the chair. "Mrs. Michaels really wanted those dolls sold so the money could be used to help others. She loved those dolls so much, and I feel I let her down in some way."

Rich continued to rub her shoulder. "I don't see why you feel you let her down. There's no reason for you to feel guilty. What happened today could've happened anywhere." He then turned to the policeman. "Officer, do you think this was a real professional hit?"

"I was just telling the ladies that, sir," the officer said, putting his hands on his hips and looking at Joy. "However, it's hard to say with an odd theft like this. Ma'am, you also mentioned that another doll dealer came into the shop today?"

She rubbed her temple. "Yes, Janet Swing came in. She's the one who asked for a referral fee if she sent me a buyer for the Ronnies."

"That old creepy bat?" Cassie interjected. "You're always telling me she rips customers off."

"So she knows a lot about the value of the dolls," Rich said, stepping back and scratching his forehead. "You didn't mention her earlier today, Joy."

"I really didn't have any need to mention her until now," she replied. "Somehow, though, I can't picture Janet stealing."

"Do you have any photos of these dolls, ma'am? I don't have any idea what a 1962 Ronnie doll looks like." The heavyset lawman folded his arms across his chest.

"Officer, I have some pictures of the dolls in

my office," Rich said, taking out a business card from his lapel pocket. "Please, come down in the morning. I'll be happy to show them to you."

After the policeman left, Cassie bent over and kissed her friend on the cheek and hugged her. "Joy, please go rest, and don't blame yourself. What happened isn't your fault." As she straightened up, she turned to Rich, "Please take her upstairs and make sure she calms down."

"Sure thing," he said as he helped Joy to her feet. She still felt numb. "Joy, let's go upstairs, and I'll make you some hot tea."

As she sat at her kitchen table sipping tea, she looked over at Rich, who would not take his eyes off her face.

"How did you know she felt she had no friends?" Joy glanced up as she asked the question.

"Mrs. Michaels was an acquaintance of my father's. Everyone talked about how she flew all over the world and attended fancy resorts after her husband died. I heard she even used to talk to her dolls because she got so lonely." Rich leaned over to hold her chin between his thumb and forefinger. "Stop the self blame, Joy."

She felt her heart flutter. His deep voice was so soothing. She wanted him to envelop her in his arms.

"Yes, she told me I was her only friend. Then one day she said she should take up other hobbies so she could meet other people. Suddenly she was diagnosed with cancer and too sick to do any of it. It was a case of realizing something too late." Joy rubbed her eyes. "I'm just sick that this should happen right before the buyer got a chance to come back for them. I really wanted to sell those two beautiful dolls to her."

"Look, Joy, don't talk about your frustrations right now. Try to concentrate on what happened before tonight. Did anyone else come into the store today?"

"No, I don't think so. I wasn't that busy." She didn't want to say she had been too busy thinking about him.

Joy took a deep breath. "I suppose I'll have to contact Mrs. Michael's estate executor as soon as possible and let him know the dolls were stolen."

"Don't do that just yet," Rich said. "Let's give ourselves a chance to find them first. Since I'll be paying out your claim, I feel an obligation to help as best I can."

She put her head in her hand. "Any other insurance company could refuse to pay, saying that I was extremely negligent in displaying those two dolls."

"What do you take me for, lady?" He knitted his brows together.

Joy smiled. "A nice guy."

Rich softly caressed her cheek. "Just don't let yourself get so worked up. People can't think rationally when they're upset. I know all about that from watching Caroline."

"I just wish I had as much faith as you do that the dolls can be found."

"Say, I've got an idea. Didn't you say the newspaper was photographing these dolls?"

Joy nodded. "Yeah, so?" She then slapped her forehead. "And I meant to call the paper to cancel the photo shoot since I'd made a tentative sale agreement."

"Good thing you didn't. I think you should tell the paper to run a caption saying that they were stolen, along with the photos."

"Rich, I'm not following your reasoning."

"Well, two dolls like that could easily be recognized from a picture," he said, steepling his hands on back of his head. "I mean, am I correct in assuming that the thief would probably try to sell them fast?"

Joy shrugged her shoulders. "It sounds rather far-fetched to think you could stop a doll thief with a photo."

"I've got a feeling the person who took the dolls is someone local." Rich turned around in his chair and crossed his legs. "However, that collector could've been staking out the place when she came in. Thieves can wear clever disguises."

"Maybe."

"Have you noticed anyone strange hanging around lately? I mean, how many people knew you had those dolls?"

"It's funny," she said hesitantly. "I don't like Janet Swing, and I'm not sure why she came in the store today. But the one person both Cassie and I have noticed hanging around on this street a lot lately is Caroline Voucher."

Rich's jaw drop several inches, and he stared at Joy in disbelief.

Chapter Twelve

He didn't know whether to laugh or shout when he heard Caroline's name. Why did he suddenly feel that this bit of news changed the entire picture of what might have happened?

"When did you see her on the street?" he asked, rising to his feet.

"Today I saw her coming out of Cassie's shop. She had an armful of flowers." Joy touched the bridge of her nose as she paused. "Cassie says she's been in her shop several times during the past week."

Rich shook his head. What was Caroline up to now? He had a bad feeling in his gut.

Joy was sitting very still. The silence was overwhelming. Then she said, "Rich, you could be right. That collector who came in could've set the stage for the robbery tonight."

He felt a wave of disgust creep over his body. "Joy, I wish I could think of some other possibility."

She stood up and moved away from the table to stand next to him. "Rich, what are you thinking now?"

"Caroline's a schemer, Joy, and a spoiled brat. She's probably been hanging around for a purpose, but I'm not sure why. I remember one time she hid her mother's jewels in her nanny's closet to get the woman fired. Of course, she never confessed to it until years later. That's why I think we may be on the right trail of the thief. But I've denied something to myself for too long, I'm afraid."

"What's that?" she asked gently, placing her hand on his forearm.

"She wants to marry me, and she's not one to relinquish something once she makes up her mind. During these months that she's been hinting around, I've just been hoping she'd quit after a while. I was sure she'd buzz off once she realized I wasn't interested."

Joy crossed her arms and stared at him.

"*I* could've told you she wanted you. I told you

what she said when she came into my shop that day. And Cassie's got bad vibes about her, too. But I just don't understand—"

"I don't either, Joy." Rich rubbed his mustache with his thumb. "But she's a manipulator, and she likes to get even with people. She's been doing that since she was a kid."

Joy rubbed her upper arms with her hands. "Would she really lie and tell me you were engaged because she saw me as a threat to what she wanted?"

"I've kidded myself into thinking she'd give up, hoping she'd eventually meet someone else. I've always regarded her as a family friend."

Rich watched Joy shake her head and throw her hands up in the air in exasperation. "Well, I don't know what to think, but I still say that Janet Swing coming in here was just too strange. I've never liked that woman, and I wonder how she heard about those two Ronnies, anyway."

"We shouldn't dismiss any possibilities yet," Rich said, pacing the floor. "But Joy, I want you to know I've never been romantically involved with a client before." He paused. "At least not until now."

"Is that how you're referring to us now, Rich?" she asked slowly. "Am I a 'romantic involvement'?"

"Well, I think 'friend' is a bit strange to call

you now. And I haven't spoken to any woman about the things I've spoken to you about."

Joy let out a laugh. "Rich Buckley, women adore men like you."

"So, my ex-wife adored me for a while too before she fell so madly in love with her own success dream," he said bitterly. "Of course, Margie had no interests outside of herself by that time."

"Do you think she was so driven because she had so few interests in life?"

"Partly, yes. I also know she felt she'd married beneath her and had to prove something to the world. I've struggled for years to try to comprehend what happened and why." He felt a crushing sensation in his chest. He couldn't believe he had finally blurted out those details to someone.

"My goodness," Joy said, chewing on her lower lip. "Here I thought you imagined *me* as some sort of gold digger."

Rich took a step closer to her. "I'm not lying to you when I say I haven't been deeply involved with anyone since, and I want you to count on me now to help you in this situation."

She reached over to put a hand on his shoulder. "Rich, you don't need to get yourself tangled up in my problem. It sounds like you've got a more serious issue on your hands now—you've got to talk to Caroline right away."

He stepped forward and grabbed her by the

shoulders, pulling her to him. His voice became heavy and low. "Maybe you're right, Joy. But right now, I can't walk out the door and leave you. I'm angry about what's happened, and I—"

"And?" she interrupted with a whisper.

Rich pulled her even closer to him. She fell against his chest. He let his mouth descend upon hers as he embraced her. Her arms wrapped around his neck instantly, and she closed her eyes.

A moment later he pulled away from her.

"Are you still afraid of a relationship and commitment?" she asked, leaning back to look up at him.

He looked away from her. "I don't know. But I do know I haven't felt this close to anyone in years—or maybe ever. I'd better go."

She followed him to the door in silence. Then he turned to her. "I'll call you tomorrow. I've got an idea."

"What sort of idea?"

"Give me a list of all the exclusive doll shop owners within a fifty mile radius. I can e-mail them and ask that they keep an eye out for those two dolls. Were there any unusual markings on the boxes?"

Joy pinched her chin. "There's a letter *M* marked in pencil on the bottom of each box to show it's property of the Michaels's estate." Then she shook her head. "Of course, the thief could've erased them by now."

"Thieves aren't usually so smart," Rich quipped. "That thief's going to cash those things in right away and probably never even look at the boxes."

Joy just gawked at him. He could tell she was at a loss for words.

Chapter Thirteen

"**J**oy, do you hear me? I said I got up all the broken glass, and I think you should call the glass repair place as soon as you can." Cassie put her coffee mug down on the counter top.

"I should've been more careful," Joy said, still staring out the front window.

"Listen, I've known you a long time, and you're always careful. Someone targeted your shop."

Joy shrugged, but said nothing. She was thinking about Rich, and how he was much more complex than any man she'd ever known.

"Joy, are you listening to me? How can you be so calm after all you've been through?" Joy knew her friend was trying to tell her she felt like she was talking to a wall.

Just then the phone rang. Joy went to answer it, noting the time on the wall clock. She should be opening the shop right now.

"Miss Smathers, did I hear your message correctly on my answering machine? Did you really say that the two dolls were stolen?"

"Yes, Mrs. Hamilton, and someone's working on finding them right now. I'll keep you posted."

Joy could hear Mrs. Hamilton crying on the other end of the phone. Was she really that upset over the disappearance of the two Ronnie dolls? Didn't this woman have anything else in her life?

"Mrs. Hamilton, please calm down. Believe me, I want those dolls found too. You'll be the first person I call if and when they're found," Joy said sympathetically.

"Do you know of anyone else who has an original 1962 Ronnie for sale?" the woman asked, still choking on tears.

"No, I don't. But I know you're disappointed."

"Please do call me when they're found. I think it's so terrible that your shop was robbed. The world is full of rotten people these days." The woman sobbed again. "That's why I keep dolls around for company. The daily news makes me depressed."

Joy rolled her eyes. This woman sounded more obsessed than Loretta Michaels had been. "Well, the police and my insurance company are working hard on this theft. I've also called the paper and asked them to run a feature about their disappearance."

"All this excitement in the last two days," the older woman said between gasps, "I'd better go take a nap. And please do call me as soon as anyone's spotted them. I'll even pay you more money to cover your recovery costs."

Joy could hear the woman choking back more tears. This woman was too genuinely distraught to have been involved in the robbery, unless she was a great actress. She felt certain about that. However, she still wasn't sure Janet Swing was innocent.

She hung up the phone slowly. "That poor woman's more upset than I."

"Sounds like someone who needs a life." Cassie grimaced and leaned back against the wall. "So, where's your knight in shinning armor, Ms. Smathers?" she asked jokingly. "I bet he's out searching every nook and cranny for those dolls." Cassie threw back her head and laughed. "Imagine, a grown man hunting down Ronnie dolls for the woman he loves."

Joy only looked at her. "I'm sorry, Cass. I just can't laugh right now."

"You've got the look of love on your face, woman," Cassie said, wagging her finger.

Yes, she was in love with Rich, wasn't she? Wasn't that the simple truth of the matter?

"Well," she said after a pregnant pause, "there's a lot of confusion growing."

"Admit you're in love, Joy."

Joy shook her head. "Maybe I'm still reluctant because I realize that what I want may not be possible for him to give. Maybe I'm not marriage material somehow. I always pick men who are afraid of commitment."

"Joy, don't say that. Larson could commit to another woman, just not to you. Remember, the right guy will commit himself to you."

"Well, Rich Buckley may not commit himself ever again, Cassie. He's had a rough life up until now, with his mother's death and one bad marriage behind him. Men don't change dramatically too easily."

Cassie tapped her friend's shoulder. "You've got to give it time, friend."

"Cassie, when I gave myself to Larson, I felt used. I want more permanence—I can't let myself get involved again without it."

"You mean you won't let yourself get *hurt* again."

The phone rang. Joy darted to the wall to answer it.

"Joy, it's Janet. I just got the most distressful phone call from Meg Hamilton. You can't really be serious! Those dolls were really taken from your shop? I thought you had good security there."

Joy closed her eyes and stifled a groan. She really didn't want to talk to Janet right now, but it was necessary.

"What can I say, Janet? I simply locked up the shop and left for a couple of hours. When I came back, they were gone."

She could hear her gasp in shock on the other end of the line.

"Well, I was at the big toy expo dinner in Baltimore last night, and I was telling people about those pristine dolls. I was even thinking how wonderful it was that you had them, and my oh my." Janet paused to cluck her tongue. "But Joy, those dolls can't have gone very far, and they're bound to turn up. I'm sure whoever stole them is going to try to sell them." Then her voice became excited. "You know, I could help send out the word cautioning all dealers that they're stolen property. Not too many people have both the blond and brunette 1962 Ronnie doll. That's highly unusual. And here I was, getting ready to spend my fee."

How could Janet be willing to help locate the dolls if she'd been the one to steal them? She seemed more concerned about her finder's fee.

"Thank you, Janet. But a friend of mine's already sending out an e-mail message."

After Joy hung up the phone, Cassie asked, "So, Joy, you never did tell me. What is Mr. Buckley's game plan for locating those dolls?"

"Oh Cass, he's going to—," she paused mid-sentence and rubbed her eyes before turning her head, "he's publicizing the theft on the Internet."

Chapter Fourteen

He shifted gears and kept his eyes on the road, thinking about how angry he was. Why was he so mad? Was he really so angry at Caroline because she might have stolen the dolls, or was he angry that someone was playing games with him? He couldn't remember feeling so outraged.

Then his thoughts shifted to Joy, and his hands began to tremble. How dare Caroline put her through such grief. No, *he* was the one who was so upset right now. He slammed his palm down on the steering wheel. Ever since the divorce, he'd prided himself on better control of his emotions.

Rich slowed down as he approached the bend in the road and saw the wrought iron gates to the Voucher estate. If he had to confront Joe Voucher today in front of his daughter, he would. He didn't care about preserving their partnership anymore.

The big gate opened after Rich announced his arrival on the intercom. He noticed that the lawns surrounding the big brick mansion were perfectly manicured.

As he walked up the large marble steps to the heavy front door, he thought about how some people didn't deserve great wealth. A small, thin maid answered the door and showed Rich into a small study room at the end of a long narrow corridor. Joe Voucher sat in a big leather wing chair with his legs crossed and a book in his lap.

"Well, Rich, what brings you here today? It's always a pleasure to see you, son. But you look troubled." The thin gray-haired man took off his glasses as he spoke.

"Well, I'm concerned about a client who was robbed," he answered, clasping his hands calmly behind his back. "Is Caroline here?"

The old man jerked his head up and said, "Well, what's the big deal about a client being robbed? We insure people for just that reason, don't we?" The old man combed a hand through his thin hair and added, "Now, Rich, I also think you know better than to get too involved with clients. I thought I warned you about it once before."

"I've always tried to be compassionate toward our clients," Rich said through clenched teeth.

"Yes, well, anyway, Caroline's out right now, but you can keep me company for lunch. I was going to go into the office in a couple of hours." The old man folded his hands in his lap. "You know, my daughter was just saying today how much she's missed you. You haven't been around lately. We haven't seen you at the club much, either."

"Well, Joe, I've had other things to do. Life does not revolve around a social club. We also have a list of loyal clients who need service and don't care about our company's expansion. I've been concentrating on meeting their special needs, while you've been investigating mergers and acquisitions. So, where is Caroline?"

Joe Voucher cleared his throat. "Caroline's off today doing work for a charity project. I don't know all the details, but you know how devoted Caroline is."

"I see," Rich replied, pacing the room. "We really need to talk to her about something, Joe."

"*We*? Good heavens, what could be so urgent?" A puzzled expression played across the man's face.

"Relax, Joe, I don't want you to stress yourself out. There's just some things we should deal with right now."

"Well, talk about being forthright," the old man snapped. "We can talk about whatever you want to over lunch. Carmen's serving crabcakes today." Joe Voucher massaged his throat as he spoke.

"Joe," Rich said shaking his head in a forlorn way and looking up at the ceiling. "I'm not sure our partnership's going well—"

"Son, you need to be more risky," his partner interrupted. "Businesses are either expanding nowadays or dying. You're a young smart guy with good sense. You and I together could build an even broader client base, making this the biggest local insurance company—"

"Joe, it's more than just that, and you know that my dad never would've agreed to this sort of rapid growth. Our customers have always been satisfied, and that's what counts."

"Rich, we'll talk about that next month after the Lane deal goes through."

Rich could hear the anger in Joe's voice. He continued to pace the room and said, "Joe, I really do need to talk to your daughter." He cleared his throat. "There's something strange going on right now that I really feel I have to talk to her about."

Joe's eyes lit up and he clapped his hands together. "Ah-ha! Well, why don't you come to the dinner she's having tonight for some of the country club set?" He shifted position in his chair and kept rambling. "I've tried to talk to you about it for the last couple of days, but you've been too busy, and I—"

"I need to talk privately with Caroline," Rich interrupted.

How could he tell Joe that his daughter was chasing after him, trying to sabotage his budding relationship with Joy? He could see from the expression on the old guy's face that Joe wanted him and Caroline to be together. He scratched his eyebrow and looked down at the ground. This meeting was not turning out as planned. Joe was not willing to consider his business viewpoint right now, either.

"I can tell Caroline to call you as soon as she gets home. But come on by tonight, son, around seven. We'd love your company." Joe Voucher leaned forward in his chair and rang the bell for the maid. "Come on, Rich. Let's have lunch." His tone of voice was jovial.

"No, I'm busy," Rich replied. Both Caroline and her father needed to see he wasn't going to play along with their wishes. "Sorry, Joe, now's not a good time to discuss business over lunch. Joy really needs my help right now."

The corners of Joe's eyes narrowed, and Rich could tell his partner was angry. His face turned white. His expression slowly changed as he asked, "Who's Joy?"

"She's the lady I was telling you about, Joe, and she's one of our clients."

Just then the maid came in with a sparkling

water for his aging partner. He took the glass between shaking fingers and put it on the table next to him. "I see. Well, I do hope she's not taking up too much of your time."

His piercing eyes made Rich uncomfortable. Joe Voucher was silent as Rich exited the small room.

"I don't know what I'm doing," he muttered as he started the car engine and turned down the long driveway out of the estate. "So why do I think Caroline took those dolls? I'm just so sure she did."

Why did he feel like he'd just been wiped out? Shouldn't he have said something more to Joe? Shouldn't he have argued more vehemently against the company's expansion?

When he came to the first stop sign along the road, he pulled over and dialed his office number on his cell phone. After his secretary answered, he said, "Listen, Jane, I'm going over to that toy shop on Main Street. The owner's been so distraught over that theft. I'll probably be there most of the day, and—"

"Mr. Buckley," Jane gasped, "some doll shop owner down in Delaware responded to the E-mail message you sent out about the missing Ronnie dolls. She said for you to call her right away."

Chapter Fifteen

"He said *what?*" Cassie squealed, jumping up and down. "He sure is a wonder, that guy."

"Well," Joy answered, rubbing her face, "he didn't have too much time to explain. But it seems that some woman just called claiming that someone walked into her shop this morning with two 1962 Ronnie dolls, demanding fair market value."

"Where is the shop?" Cassie asked, shaking her head incredulously.

"Somewhere over the Delaware border," Joy said, folding her arms and leaning against the counter. "Rich is on his way over right now. He got directions and says it's about two and a half hours away."

"I'll watch the shop for you, and—"

"Hi there," a male voice bellowed over Cassie's as the shop door opened.

"Rich, you're amazing," Cassie said, racing over to give him a kiss on the cheek.

Joy saw Rich's face redden at Cassie's exuberence. He simply smiled. "You ready to go, Joy?" he asked, draping an arm over the register.

"You bet she is," Cassie quipped. "But not until I hear some more details. I'm going to pace the floor 'til you both get back. Who's this woman, Rich? They couldn't have *that* many first edition Ronnie dolls circulating out there. I find all that's happened so far incredible."

"I want a good description of who brought in those dolls," Joy added, slinging her handbag over her shoulder.

"Don't worry. We'll find out everything in a couple of hours. But this woman only gave a vague description over the phone."

Joy's eyes met Rich's. She saw anger mixed with curiosity. Was he afraid of what they'd learn from the shop owner?

"Let's go," he muttered, walking toward the door.

They rode silently in the car for over an hour. Joy thought the stillness was uncomfortable until he reached over to pat her hand, never taking his eyes off the road.

She felt something powerful pulling them together right now, but would it last? Could she fit into his narrow, monied, conservative world? Would she be able to just enjoy a fling with him and move on when it was over? *No.* One mistake in a lifetime was enough.

It had been too long since she felt loved. There was no point in denying it. She had to confront those feelings. Whatever would keep Rich from her probably had little to do with Caroline Voucher.

However, she couldn't blame Caroline for wanting Rich so badly. He was rich, handsome, thoughtful, and young at heart.

Her thoughts were interrupted by his voice.

"I know you're nervous, but—"

"Rich," she interrupted, "what if the thief erased the letter *M* I drew on the boxes? I'll never be able to claim them then."

"Joy, everything's going to work out. It'll be fine. I'll make sure it is."

She felt a lump forming in her throat. What did he mean? If only he could always be there to make everything go smoothly in her life.

It was dark when they pulled in to the parking lot of the *Doll Palace*. The gray stucco building had a large illuminated sign out front that said *Closed*.

Joy let out a deep breath as Rich circled the

parking lot. Then a plump figure appeared in the shop's window. Within seconds, lights flooded the vacant lot. Joy did not take her eyes from the front door as it slowly opened. A middle-aged woman with short black and gray streaked hair smiled and waved to them.

"You're here about the dolls, right?" she called out.

Joy leaped out of the car. "Do you really have both of them, the blond and the brunet?"

"Yes, dear, come in and I'll show you. I'm sure they must be yours." The woman motioned with her hand for them to come inside.

Rich slammed the car door shut. "Who'd have believed that there'd still be such an honest person left in this world?"

As they stepped inside, the jolly owner extended her hand to Joy. "I'm Doris Leach, and I'm so glad I could be of assistance. I should've questioned the woman who brought them in this morning."

"Can you describe her?" Rich asked, stepping forward with his hands on his hips.

"Well, she was thin and wore a jean jacket and a big floppy hat," Doris said, gesticulating with her hands. "She also wore sunglasses and had a deep husky voice."

"What did she tell you about these dolls?" Joy asked eagerly.

"She simply said she'd been cleaning out the closets of an elderly aunt and came upon them in a suitcase." Doris Leach then shook her head. Moving behind the counter, she wiped her hands on her flowered shift.

Joy glanced around the *Doll Palace* noting how clean it was. This woman had shelves full of every doll imaginable, and there was no glass covering them. However, she could not see a single speck of dust on the dolls' dresses. The carpet on the floor was worn but dirt free.

Doris bent down behind the counter and took out two old Ronnie doll boxes. She lay them on the counter side by side. As she stepped closer to look at the dolls, Joy felt her heart race. On the side of one box she saw a faded letter *M*.

"I recognize them, Doris. I know they're the ones." She reached over and picked up the box containing the blond Ronnie doll and pointed to the *M* penciled faintly on the side. "This doll came from the estate of my friend, whose last name was Michaels. I penciled that there for inventory purposes."

Doris nodded and winked at her.

"Miss Leach," Rich said after clearing his throat and stepping forward, "what color hair did this woman have?"

"Well, that's just it. Her hair was tucked up inside the hat, and I couldn't see what color it was." Doris paused to think, laying a finger on the side of her nose. "I really can't say I looked at her too closely. She seemed in a real hurry to get the money. She didn't even care when I told her I could only pay her a fraction of the dolls' market value; she just wanted cash."

"So, how much did you pay her?" Joy asked.

"Only a couple thousand. I told her that I'd split the difference with her once I sold them. So she agreed to take the retainer since it was all I could give her." Doris sighed. "I should've thought about it, though, because I did think it was all a bit strange. However, I never considered the possibility they were stolen property."

"Doris, I'll make sure you get back the money you paid her once I sell these dolls."

"But I do remember one thing," Doris said, "her car sure did make a lot of loud noise."

Joy turned to stare at Rich, whose jaw had just dropped.

Chapter Sixteen

Rich felt a drop of sweat roll down his face. His hands tightened on the steering wheel as he pulled over to the curb to let Joy out. He then turned off the ignition and drummed his fingers on the dashboard.

"Rich," Joy said softly, reaching over to touch his hand, "you've been so tense driving back. Relax, we got the dolls back." She let out a deep breath. "I think we should call it a night, and—"

"I've got to confront her, Joy. She did this for some diabolical reason, and I've got to get to the bottom of it," he interrupted, turning to face her.

She swallowed before saying, "I think I'm the one to confront her. She's got it in for me, and I don't like people who play around with my head."

After Rich grunted, she added, "I know she's your partner's daughter, and you've got a lot at stake in your relationship with the family."

"I've got plenty to say to her myself," Rich grumbled.

"Rich, please," Joy pleaded.

"We'll talk later, Joy. Good night," he muttered. "Oh, and Joy," he added as she stepped out of the car, "don't tell anyone you found those dolls just yet."

Rich turned on the computer switch and massaged his forehead. He sure needed a cup of coffee right now. He glanced at his watch. It was eight-thirty in the morning.

A knock on his office door jolted his senses. He spun around to see Joe Voucher leaning against the doorwell. His gray hair was slicked back, emphasizing the lines in his face.

"You look worn out, Rich," he quipped. "Maybe you've been putting in too many hours."

"Yeah, well I was up late last night," he said, stretching his arms and then walked over to sit down at his desk. "So what's up, Joe?"

"Well," Joe said, sitting down in the chair across from him, "I came to tell you the good news."

"What good news?"

"Somehow Caroline's managed to get together

enough money to start her own law office in the center of town." Joe could not hide the pride in his voice.

"Really?" Rich said, raising an eyebrow as he leaned forward.

"Oh yes. She's given notice and is leaving her job today," Joe said eagerly. "So I thought it would be nice to have a little surprise party at the club for her this afternoon to celebrate."

"And?" Rich asked, cocking his head to one side.

"The party will start at noon. I want all of her closest friends to come. You should be there." Joe let out a hoarse chuckle. "She's something, that little girl of mine, isn't she? And she's really determined to make it in the world. I think she's as smart and ambitious as your ex-wife Margie was. You know, she deserves the best." Joe Voucher folded his hands and smiled.

Rich sat speechless. Just then the phone rang, and he pressed a thumb down on the intercom key.

"Sir, Miss Smathers is here to see you," his secretary said.

"Send her in," he mumbled.

"Rich," Joe Voucher stammered angrily, rising from his chair, "I was not finished speaking to you about Caroline."

Rich slowly rose from the desk chair and leaned forward. "Joe, I think—"

"Hello," Joy said, "I hope I'm not interrupting anything."

Joe Voucher turned to glare at her before saying, "Rich, I do hope you'll come this afternoon. I know it would mean a lot to Caroline if you were there for the celebration."

"Joe, this is Joy Smathers, one of our clients. Joy, meet my partner, Joe Voucher." Rich turned his head to look at Joy as she nodded in greeting. "You're not busy this afternoon, are you?" he asked, motioning for her to sit down. "If you could get someone to look after the shop, I'd like you to come to Caroline's party with me." He saw Joe Voucher's face twist in anger, but the older man was too exasperated to speak. "Okay, well, Joy and I will be there this afternoon, then."

"But Caroline—"

"Joy and I have things to discuss, Joe. You and I can talk privately later," Rich interrupted, as Joy sat down in a nearby chair. "Goodbye Joe."

"Now what was that all about?" Joy asked after Joe left the room.

Rich let out a low whistle. "I need for you to come to this surprise party with me. You won't believe what I just found out."

*   *   *

He took her arm and escorted her up the drive to the front porch of the enormous clubhouse. The scent of garden flowers pleasantly assaulted her nostrils. Joy looked around for Caroline among the elegant crowd on the terrace.

She appeared a few minutes later in the doorway, holding onto her father's arm. Her white linen suit was beautiful, and complimented her dark tan. The straight blond hair was perfectly coifed in a lovely French twist. But Caroline's expression changed when she saw Rich and Joy approaching.

"Well, Rich, how lovely to see you," Joe Voucher said, stepping forward to shake his hand. "And Joy came, I see." The older man arched his brow at her as he extended his hand, but there was no enthusiasm in his voice at all.

"Nice party, Joe," Rich muttered in a casual but guarded tone. Joy couldn't help but notice how uneasy they were with each other.

Caroline gave Rich an icy stare.

"Miss, I'm so sorry to hear that your shop was robbed. Surely Rich'll see to it that you're compensated as quickly as possible." Joe Voucher cleared his throat and shifted position as he put his arms behind his back.

Joy glanced to the left. For some reason she didn't want to see Caroline's reaction to the last comment.

"Thank you, sir."

Caroline let out a small gasp, but it seemed to come too late. "Why, that's terrible. I guess that's what comes from overpricing small items." Then she laughed. "I can't imagine why anyone would want those two ugly dolls so badly they'd steal them. It must be a real nut who took them, but then aren't all your customers a little weird, Joy?"

Rich made no sound. Joy only swallowed.

"Well, Caroline, congratulations on your new practice," Rich said, stuffing his hands in his trouser pockets.

"Yes, she sure is amazing, isn't she!" Joe Voucher exclaimed.

"I think it's interesting that you want to practice law on your own, Caroline," Joy said slowly. "I would think it's hard to get started."

Caroline suddenly excused herself. "I must go see to our guests inside, Father."

Joe Voucher cleared his throat and looked at Joy directly. "Mrs. Michaels was a rather flamboyant character as I recall. I think dolls were her only great love in life."

Joy nodded. She was not going to let this snobby man look down on her.

"She did admit that to me once."

"I don't imagine that old bat probably had many friends besides you," Joe Voucher said with a laugh.

Joy then glanced over at Caroline, who was flitting from guest to guest in an animated fashion. She was now playing the part of the perfect party hostess.

Joe Voucher continued to ramble. "So, why are you two here together today?"

"Well, I want Joy to get to know as many people here as possible," Rich answered, touching her elbow.

Joy knew this man did not like the fact that the two of them had come together.

"I find people who collect dolls as adults very odd," Joe Voucher said, crossing his arms.

"Joy, let's go get something to eat. I see you got them to lay out a great spread inside, Joe," Rich said, pointing to the buffet table near the wall inside the door. He then grabbed Joy's arm, pulling her inside.

"You know, Rich, Caroline will make a wonderful wife for some lucky man one day," Joe called to his back as they walked away. "You should sample her cooking some time."

Joy rolled her eyes at the last remark. Rich didn't answer. He just headed toward the bar which was set up in the corner of the clubhouse room.

"What'll you have?" the bartender asked.

"Water, my throat's dry," Joy snapped. Rich looked stunned.

"Joy, don't you think that's a bit strong for the occasion?" he chuckled, nervously patting her shoulder.

"My nerves are shot after that insane conversation," Joy said, leaning against the bar.

"Don't let him get to you. Joe Voucher's simply a little strange."

"The entire conversation was stupid," she quipped in disgust. "Look, I snap when I get angry like I am right now. So take it or leave it, Rich."

"You don't have to work with him all day like I do," Rich whispered in her ear as he stepped closer to the bar.

They stood side by side in silence as the bartender put two glasses of water down in front of them. Joy immediately grabbed the glass and took two long swallows.

"Are you implying that I don't have to work as hard as you do all day?"

"Whoa, Joy, cool down a bit." He reached over and grasped her wrist, pulling her closer to him. His voice lowered. "Look, I know we're in the midst of an embarrassing situation, but we can handle this."

"Why, Rich Buckley, it's so good to see you," a thin elderly woman exclaimed, opening up her arms to embrace him as she approached.

"Hello, Mrs. Cornwallis, how's your antique business coming along?" Rich asked pleasantly.

"I've been doing just fine. I was wondering when you're going to stop back and visit me. I've expanded the business, and I need to upgrade my policy."

Rich nodded. "Mrs. Cornwallis, please meet Joy Smathers."

Joy extended her hand. "I've passed your antiques gallery a few times and seen your lovely window displays."

"Why, thank you," Mrs. Cornwallis said, brushing back a lock of gray hair. "You're a client of Buckley and Voucher too, I take it? Do you own that lovely collectibles shop that's selling Mrs. Michaels's doll collection?"

Both Joy and Rich nodded. Mrs. Cornwallis went on and on about her own shop, and Joy casually let her gaze wander over to Caroline. She was avoiding the two of them at all costs. Her eyes met Joy's a few times, but she could not make out the expression on her face. Was she angry, sad or hurt?

"So, are porcelain dolls from the turn of the century a big selling item these days?" Mrs. Cornwallis asked.

"Were you thinking of selling them?" Joy asked. "Because if you are, I must caution you that doll values go up and down according to the preferences of the collectors' market, so values don't remain constant."

"Your job must be fascinating, Miss Smathers." The older woman smiled warmly at her.

"I do have interesting clients who collect for all sorts of reasons. Although I only advocate pleasure as the reason to collect—collectible toys are not a sound investment."

Joy's gaze shifted to Rich, who had meandered over to the corner of the room. His arms were crossed in front of his chest, and he was tapping his foot. The look on his face was tense. She excused herself from Mrs. Cornwallis, put her glass down on a nearby table and walked over to the corner.

"Rich, I—"

"You know what really galls me?" he interrupted, running a hand through his hair. "She's setting up her own legal practice after *she's* just broken the law." He shook his head incredulously.

"I know," she replied, "But I'm the one who should press charges, and—"

"It wouldn't be worth it," he interjected. "Her father would protect her to the hilt." He scratched the back of his neck. "But I can't leave here without giving her a piece of my mind." Letting out a deep breath, he walked away.

She watched him approach Caroline. He pointed to a side door leading out to a vacant spot on the terrace. Caroline followed him outside. Joy felt her heart pound. What was he going to say to her?

She bolted toward the door leading out onto the porch, panic rising like bile in her throat. She heard Rich shouting and saw him standing there pointing a finger at Caroline.

"Caroline, I know it was you. How *could* you?"

Caroline stood with her hands clenched at her sides. She was shaking her head frantically from side to side.

"Your car muffler gave you away," Rich continued. "It has a distinct loud sound. I knew it was you, from the way Miss Leach described the car's noise."

"Mrs. Michaels introduced you to Margie at the club years ago. Nobody should be giving money to cancer research in her name." Caroline did not take her eyes off him.

"Caroline, why did you really do it?" Joy asked, stepping forward. "Did you really need the money to set up your own law office that badly?"

Joy could see the fury in her eyes now. The woman's shoulders were shaking.

"Don't you realize you could be disbarred if charges are brought against you?" Rich asked.

"I stole for *you*!" Caroline screeched at the top of her lungs. "I know I can be just as successful as Margie was, and I know I can make you love me as much as you loved her."

"There's nothing admirable in robbery, Caroline. Crime achieves nothing." Joy's voice remained steady as she spoke.

"I hate how Margie took you away from me," Caroline wailed. "She doesn't understand." Caroline pointed to Joy. "How can you find someone like her so appealing now? What has she got that I don't?"

"Caroline, cut it out," Rich said, turning his back to her. "Don't you see there never was an us."

"She's not good enough for you!" Caroline screamed, pointing at Joy.

"And you need psychiatric help." Rich did not move, just looked at the ground.

"I'm a good person, Rich. You can't end up with her. I've loved you for years!" She clasped her hands together pleadingly. "Rich, I made so many plans for us."

"Caroline, what plans?"

"Rich, you've always said that our lives were entangled together. I never stopped loving you all those years you were married." She wiped her tears away with the back of her hand. "I'd be so much better for you than Margie was."

"Caroline, come on now. We grew up together;

that's why our lives are intertwined. You need to get a life of your own," he said, stepping away from her.

"She's not worthy of you, Rich," Caroline wailed. "Tell me what you want. I'll give it to you."

"I want nothing. I can't marry you," he said, shaking his head in disgust. "I refuse to be miserable again. Margie destroyed any illusions I had about marriage."

Joy stood next to the door feeling her chest tighten. So what she'd thought was true—he wanted only to live alone now. He was still hung up on his ex-wife. She'd heard it now with her own two ears.

"Rich, you've got to listen to me," Caroline whimpered as she paced back and forth, wringing her hands.

"No, Caroline, you need help. You can't go through life deceiving yourself like this." He drew in his breath before moving toward Joy.

"Let's go," he said, taking her hand.

They walked silently to the club entrance. Joe Voucher stood near the door with a strained look on his face. Had he heard all the commotion?

"Thanks a lot, Joe," Rich said sadly. "We'll talk at the office tomorrow. I think you need to go see your daughter right now."

"What's going on? Why are you leaving so

soon, Rich? The party's just getting started." Joe took a step forward, clutching a drink in his hand, but his fingers were trembling.

"Joe, I need to go, and your daughter is very upset. Go talk with her," Rich said over his shoulder as he walked away.

Joy heard him clear his throat as she followed Rich out to the car. Right now, the tension was so thick one could cut it with a knife.

He stopped at the car and turned to Joy, giving her shoulders a tight squeeze. She reluctantly smiled at him, but did not say a word. He opened the car door for her.

"That woman's a piece of work," he muttered, climbing into the driver's seat.

"She's troubled, Rich, and needs help. Sometimes we just don't see the faults of the people closest to us," Joy replied, looking out the car window.

"I still can't believe it somehow. Some people can really let their feelings get the better of them." He gazed at the road ahead.

"What are you saying?" Joy asked, staring at him.

"I don't know. Joy, you've had a bee in your bonnet all night. Now out with it—are you angry with me about something?"

"What sort of game have you been playing, Rich?" After a pregnant pause, she continued, "I guess I took some signals and heart-to-heart talks we had the wrong way." She sat back in the seat and crossed both her arms and legs.

"What?"

"You just admitted you don't want a permanent relationship in your life because of Margie. So where have our talks been leading? I'm confused."

"Well, I thought we had obvious chemistry between us." He pulled the car over to side of the road. "What's up?"

"I don't think you're a bad person, Rich. However, I'm not into casual flings. I've been burned before, and I guess I can't see any purpose to our courtship now." She let out a deep breath and gazed out the window. She couldn't believe she'd really just blurted out what was on her mind.

"Did I embarrass you tonight, Joy? I just don't understand why you're so angry with me." He had turned the ignition off and shifted his body to face her.

"Rich, let's not play games here. We just have to admit that we're not suited to one other. This will never work."

"How can you say that after all we've experienced together? I don't believe you, Joy." He slapped the palm of his hand against his forehead and squeezed his eyes shut.

"I appreciate all of your help in getting the dolls

back. But if we keep seeing each other, it's going to lead to a place that it shouldn't for me."

He turned to look out the window.

"Yeah, right. I guess so."

"Look, we don't want the same things. We've just got an attraction here; let's not lose our heads over it."

"You're sure you really feel that way?" he asked in a low deep voice.

"Yes, and I'll walk myself home now. The center of town isn't far from here. Thanks for helping me find those dolls. I would never have gotten them back without you." She opened the passenger side door and stepped out.

"Yeah, right. You're welcome," he called out the window. "You know, I really stuck my neck out for you."

Joy had her back to him. She was about to go, but she could not move. She bit her lower lip to hold back tears. "I know you did, and I'll always be grateful to you for that. I do hope you can still have some sort of relationship with your partner after this."

She shielded her eyes with her hand, and walked up to the main road. What had she just done? Why did she feel this heavy sinking feeling in her heart? It just didn't make any sense. She knew that as soon as she got home, she would throw herself onto the bed and cry herself to sleep.

Chapter Seventeen

Joy hugged her sweater to her body and looked out the shop window as she took a sip of hot coffee, though she could barely taste it. Hadn't she read somewhere that depression dulled the senses? Maybe she should go see a therapist. She hadn't felt well in weeks.

She looked down at the cash drawer of the register. She couldn't complain about business. Sales had really increased ever since the theft had made news in the local paper. Of course, the dedication to the Cancer Foundation had helped too. Meg Hamilton had not only bought the two Ronnie dolls, but she had sent Joy several customers as well. However, the cash flow did nothing to lift her spirits. Why did she feel so hollow inside?

"I've never seen anyone look so depressed while counting money. You look dead," Cassie said as she walked in the door.

Joy sighed. "Sorry, Cassie. I'm just not in a good mood today. And I know I should snap out of it, but I don't know how."

"What else is new?" Cassie's tone was sarcastic. "You've been down in the dumps since the last full moon. You haven't even gone anywhere since—"

Joy shot her a dirty look that halted her midsentence. She didn't want to remember that party for Caroline.

"Joy," Cassie continued with a serious look on her face, "I really think you should do as I say. Talk to a counselor."

"Talk to a counselor about what? I thought I really was on to something special with Rich Buckley. Then I realized I made a mistake. I don't think there's anything anyone can say to me except that I was wrong."

"Oh, Joy, we all make mistakes. We all have to take chances in life. You can't let what's happened keep you in a funk forever."

"Yes, I know. But, Cassie, I keep making the same mistakes over and over again. Is a counselor really going to be able to tell me why I keep falling in love with the wrong men? I don't think there's any reason except bad choices."

Cassie frowned. "Who knows. But Joy, you've got to do *something*."

"Maybe the truth is that I'd be better off living life as a spinster. Maybe my expectations are too high." She cringed at the sound of self-pity in her own voice.

"Are they?" Cassie's voice was very soft. "If you strongly feel that way, then you definitely need to see a therapist, because your walk doesn't match your talk right now."

"I suppose you're right, but I've got nothing to say to anyone. You're a good friend to put up with me, because I know I've been a pain lately."

"Oh, stop acting like a charity case. This too shall pass, dear friend."

"Yeah, you're probably right," Joy mumbled under her breath. However, she wasn't sure Cassie's last remark was correct. She didn't know if she ever would feel okay again. She hadn't been this depressed even after her break-up with Larson.

Cassie was about to make another comment when the phone rang. Joy answered it.

"Miss Smathers?" asked an unfamiliar voice on the other end of the phone. "I understand that you do appraisals of old toy trains."

"Yes indeed, sir. However, I do charge a small fee for my time. Did you want to set up an appointment?"

"Well, I expected to pay a fee. I also understand that your store is very impressive. I've heard you have some really nice train sets."

"Why, yes. I do have a few," Joy paused. "Are you looking for something in particular?"

"Well, I don't know. I just wanted to look. My old friend Rich Buckley told me all about you and your shop. And I have a very large collection, and I thought—"

"I see," she interrupted. *Rich Buckley! Why did he have to mention him of all people?*

She didn't hear any more of what he said. She was almost in a trance. Then she stuttered as she tried to find the words, "Well, Mr.—I'm sorry, I didn't catch your name."

"Mr. Bruce," he replied. "Will you be open tomorrow around five-fifteen in the afternoon?"

"Sure thing," she answered, looking over at Cassie with a helpless look on her face.

"Well, we'll see you tomorrow, Miss Smathers. Looking forward to it."

"Great," she said as she hung up the phone. "Cassie, you won't believe this. Some train fanatic friend of Rich Buckley's is coming over for an appraisal. He also wants to see some sets."

Cassie gasped and jumped. "I bet Rich is sending him because he doesn't have the nerve to face you. He's sending this guy to spy on you."

"Cassie, don't be stupid. He sounds like a genuine collector, if you ask me."

"Why do you think he mentioned Rich?"

Joy shrugged and moved over to the porcelain doll display case. She started fluffing a doll's hair. "I don't know," she said.

"Well, Rich, it's done. But I still want to know why you can't call this woman and tell her you'd like to buy those trains yourself." Al Bruce rubbed his eyes and smoothed his red hair.

"Like I said, Al, it's not really any of your business, okay? I have my reasons." He paused and got up from his chair, walking to the window with his hands in his pockets. He turned to look down at the street below. "I'm just curious about those train sets. I've had my eye on them and I was interested in buying them."

"Sure you were. Rich, what is up with you and this broad?" Al Bruce could not hide the amusement in his voice.

He regretted letting Joy walk away from him that night. Was he such a coward that he couldn't try to talk to her at all? He hadn't slept well for weeks.

"This chick must be something, if she had that sort of effect on him. What do you say, Al?" Rich looked over to see James Pyle walk into his office and place a file folder on his desk. "Sorry, I couldn't help but overhear the conversation."

Rich let out a deep breath. "Look, Pyle, mind your own business. I didn't ask for comments from the peanut gallery."

As James walked away, Al snickered.

"I knew there was something different about this woman you described. You've always said you don't want involvement, yet you're ticked off that she told you to take a hike. Something's not in sync here."

Rich bit his tongue and looked out the window. Boy, Al could really bother him sometimes. He should never have involved his old chum.

"That silly wife of yours really did a number on you, pal," Al said, steepling his fingers behind his head. He leaned back in the chair across from Rich's desk.

"That's the only thing you've gotten right so far," Rich said, turning around to glare at him.

"What?"

"That Margie was shallow." Rich moved over to his desk. "And you know that I don't buy that true love nonsense, and I ain't marrying again for just that reason."

Al laughed. "Who's talking marriage, but you? We were talking about physical attraction earlier."

"Right," Rich said, moving the file folder to the corner.

Al just doubled over in the chair with laughter.

"You're something, Rich. Where is your head?"

"Look, all I've asked you to do is be a pal. I don't need your ribbing, okay?"

"Hey, man, take it easy. I just don't get what the game plan is here." Al bent over in the chair and put his elbows on his knees. "I mean, what am I supposed to do next? Ask this chick out and find out what she really thinks about you, after I buy the train set? Am I supposed to hint something to her during the transaction?"

"No," Rich snapped. "Al, just go in and buy this set for me. Then set up an appointment for her to come to your place for an appraisal. That's all." He didn't want to tell Al right now that he wanted to ask Joy a few questions, and that he'd be at Al's house when she showed up to appraise the trains.

"This is really weird, Rich," Al said, crossing his arms. "I mean, she's going to think this is really weird."

"Well, like I said earlier—you shouldn't have told her that you knew me." Al could be so dense.

"Rich, I know your marriage to Margie was bad, and I understand why you've sworn away from serious relationships. But you've been alone too long now, and you can't hide from intimacy all your life." Al cocked his head to one side as he spoke.

"Al, I don't need a lecture, and you don't know how bad my marriage was," Rich said. "I never told you half of it."

"What, that she thought you were unworthy of her?"

Rich stared at him speechless.

"I know that, and I don't blame you for being angry all these years. And yes, Caroline Voucher's a witch too. I tried to tell you for years that she wanted to hook her claws into you and you should stay away. She's a lot like Margie, in a way. But you're sorry about something that happened with this woman."

"I've nothing to be sorry about," Rich snapped.

"Well, maybe she's got a good reason to not want to see you again."

"Yeah, I told you—she wants the whole nine yards. Marriage, kids, the works, not just dating." Rich rolled his eyes in frustration.

"And you're scared because you really want a family too. Or has that changed?"

"No!" Rich shouted, rising to his feet and leaning across the desk. Then he paused and looked down. "I don't know."

"Well, why are you so concerned about what *she's* thinking right now?" Al asked, raising his shoulders.

"Look, Al, I just want to find out a few things, that's all. Let's go get dinner."

"Okay. How about the place down the street?" Al started to get up from his chair.

"Yeah, I've done enough work for one day."

"You know what's happening now? You're confused because you've always assumed you could never fall in love again." Al patted Rich on the back.

As the two men walked into the front office, James rose to his feet. "Rich, I wouldn't go just yet. Joe Voucher just called and said he really needs to talk to you ASAP. He said he's having his chauffeur bring him over right now, so you shouldn't go home yet."

Rich turned and looked at Al in disgust. "Al, you go down to the restaurant. I'll be there as soon as I can get away from here. I won't be long."

He hadn't said anything to Joe for weeks. They'd both been avoiding each other.

"Sure thing. Just don't let that old crow talk your ear off all night," Al said, turning to leave.

Rich then turned to James. "James, did he say what he wanted?"

"No, but he didn't sound too happy. In fact he sounded mad." James slung his suit jacket over his shoulder and headed for the door. "I'm glad he's your partner and not mine."

Chapter Eighteen

"I'm afraid this is not a very friendly meeting, Richard," Joe Voucher said as he took a seat opposite Rich's desk. "I'm afraid I have some very bad news."

Rich acted as though he did not hear him correctly. "Well, I can take bad news, but did you talk to Caroline?" He leaned forward on his elbows and folded his hands on the desk.

"Yes, but I'm not here to discuss my daughter." Joe Voucher coughed. "I'm afraid we're going to have to disband. We can't work together anymore. You don't respect my decisions, and I feel now is the best time to part ways."

Rich was silent. He only nodded his head in affirmation. He knew what Joe was saying was true; he didn't think they were meant to work together, either. However, he never thought Joe would break up Buckley and Voucher. Rich now realized he hadn't wanted to seriously confront Joe about it, primarily because he didn't have any other options open to him. This company had been the central focus of his life since childhood.

"You know, Rich, I had the deepest respect and admiration for your father. He was an ambitious man. But I don't think he would approve of your business sense, or your lifestyle, for that matter. Your father knew you'd made a terrible mistake marrying that fortune hunter, Margie Ross, but now you've shown you've got no sense at all in your personal life."

"Are you telling me you're breaking up this partnership because I won't marry your daughter?"

The older man crossed his legs and looked down at the floor. "No, not entirely. Although I must say I am disappointed. You know, your parents, and my wife and I always thought the two of you would marry one day, in spite of the difference in your ages. You two always played so well together as children."

The old man gripped the arm of the chair as Rich grunted in disgust. Rich felt angry, but he had a very heavy feeling in his chest. He didn't know if it was nerves or fear. So what did he have left in his life right now?

"The two of you are ideally suited to each other," Joe continued. "I mean, you both have the same sort of breeding and upbringing. That female you brought to the club wouldn't fit—"

"I really don't see who you are to judge other people," Rich interrupted. "You're nothing but a typical snob. Do you care about nothing else in life? You're going to just break up the company and throw years of toil down the drain? Don't you care about what sort of legacy you're leaving to your children and grandchildren? Or how our customers will feel if this goes through?" He ran a hand through his hair.

"Oh, I've already thought of it. I intend to start a new insurance company. I'll be taking most of the accounts, since most of our clients know me better than you."

Rich's jaw dropped. He looked at the heartless man in front of him. Could his father ever really have been good friends with Joe? He was so petty and childish.

"Well then, this is good-bye. This is the end of the company. Remember, all the money and the hard work that started this business was not all yours. It was my family's, too. I think you're acting rash. We don't have to be bosom buddies to be in business together."

The old man coughed again. "I don't think I'm being too hasty in my decision."

Rich chuckled. "Fine, Joe. You know, you're not going to ruin me. I won't let you or anyone else do that."

"We should be civilized when dividing the assets. Caroline's going to be my new partner. She needs to get involved with the business."

Rich squeezed his eyes shut and grinned. "How nice for you, Joe. I've got nothing else to say, I just have to think things over. Tell me one thing, though: what are you going to do about our employees? Are you taking them with you, too?" Rich's heart almost stopped beating when he thought of the people who had worked so hard for Buckley and Voucher.

"I don't know, but I'm not going to tell them anything. I expect you to do it. I may offer one or two of them a job with my new company, but otherwise, I really feel they're your responsibility. You've been managing this office, not me."

Rich felt his ears burn. Should he tell the guy his daughter was a thief? Did this man ever think about anyone but himself? If he really loved his daughter, he wouldn't want her to marry a man who didn't love her. He now regretted all those times he'd bitten his tongue with Joe. He'd always told himself he shouldn't ruin the relationship with his father's partner, but obvious friendship and loyalty meant nothing here.

Joe Voucher was about to say something else, but Rich waved his hand in the air to cut him off. "Joe, just go. We've said all there is to say."

He needed to talk to Al. No, he really wished he could talk to Joy. She would understand and give him good suggestions, because she'd lived through lean times when starting her own business from scratch.

Life sure could be hard. Especially when you were living it all alone. Did he really want to live out his days by himself, after all? Life seemed so empty right now. He had no parents now, but they had always been proud of his accomplishments. But now he had only a handful of friends and a large bag of bad memories.

"Well, isn't failure the first step toward success? Isn't that what Granddad always said?" Rich asked aloud. But it was up to him to take the next step, and to make sure it was in the right direction.

Chapter Nineteen

"Ms. Smathers, your shop is fantastic," the red-haired man in the Italian suit said. Joy just glanced at him, barely able to utter a word. "I also like your window displays. You know, my niece has been wanting a Chez doll. I'll have to pick out one for her before I leave," he added.

"If you buy a lot today, Mr. Bruce, I'll give you a discount on the doll." She grinned. "I like to keep good customers coming back."

"You know, those train sets over there really are in good condition. Rich loved toy trains when we were kids." He paused to scratch his chin and gaze into the case against the wall. "Name your price for these three train sets here, Ms. Smathers. I'll take them all."

Joy was surprised by his quick decision. She liked this man's sophisticated air, but was leery of him since he'd said he was Rich Buckley's friend. "Wouldn't you like to see them and get a better look?"

He laughed. "I have it on good authority that you're an excellent dealer, Ms. Smathers. I trust you." He reached into his jacket pocket and took out a check book.

"Well, Mr. Bruce, I certainly am flattered by your confidence in me. However, I'm curious as to why you're so certain so soon." She opened the cash register as he wrote out his check.

"Rich Buckley described these sets perfectly. He knew what I was looking for, and I trust Rich's judgment. You know, he also described you to a T, I might add."

"Did he?" Joy asked, rubbing her cheek. Should she ask what Rich Buckley had said about her?

"Yes. Now tell me, could you please box up these sets?" After Joy nodded her head, he added, "I'd also like that blond Chez doll there." When she turned her back to go to the window, he asked, "I was hoping you could come to my house to see my train collection this Sunday. I'm sure I have some pieces that have gone up in value, and I want an expert's assessment."

Joy frowned. She rarely went to people's houses to do appraisals. "I really don't like to move my trains. I worry about pieces getting lost," he winked at her as he spoke.

"Oh, sure. I understand," Joy said.

Al Bruce smiled. "I will double your appraisal fee for your housecall." His eyebrows raised when he said, "I'll also provide lunch."

"Oh, that's not necessary." She turned back to the glass case near the register.

"Oh, but I insist. Is it settled then? You must come this Sunday afternoon." He slapped his hand to the counter in a gesture of finality. "Give me a pen so I can write down my address."

As Joy quoted him the final bill in thousands of dollars, he did not even react. He simply handed her a check.

"You know, Ms. Smathers, I think some things are a question of fate. I've passed your store many times, but never bothered to come inside. Now, I find it strange that I'm buying train sets from a woman who's had such an impact on my friend's personal life."

"Oh?" Joy asked as she gave him his receipt.

The man narrowed his left eye. "Yes, indeed. For one thing, he's really gotten into trains as a hobby. I think he needed other interests in his life."

"Yes, I remember talking to him about that." Joy rubbed her temple. She felt confused now. That was *one* thing she'd done—rekindled his interest in trains. Or had she possibly changed his life in some other way? Al Bruce sure made it sound like she had.

"Well, he certainly had a lot of flattering things to say about you."

Joy kept quiet, as she thought she shouldn't ask him anything more. "I'll see you on Sunday, Mr. Bruce," she said, handing him the boxes and the doll.

"Yes, you can't miss my place. It's right in back of the country club." Mr. Bruce turned to go after giving Joy another friendly grin.

"Oh, so you know I've been there. What did Rich tell you about the times I went there with him?" she asked, cocking her head to one side.

Mr. Bruce stopped in his tracks and turned around to stare at her. "Well, I'm afraid I heard everything that happened with Caroline. Unfortunately, Caroline's one woman who needs to get a life."

"Yeah, well, I'm sorry about the nasty scene at that little party, but Rich had to confront her at some point." Joy stepped back from the register and raised her shoulders in a forlorn gesture.

"Oh sure, although it's unfortunate that it cost Rich his partnership with Joe Voucher." Mr. Bruce shrugged and waved his hand good-bye.

"Cost him the *business*?" Joy gasped.

Mr. Bruce turned back half-way through the

door. "Yeah. Dear old Mr. Voucher said he wanted to break up the business because he didn't feel he could work with Rich anymore."

Joy's jaw dropped as she put a hand on her forehead. "You're kidding! What's he going to do now? His father started that business."

"And now Rich will have to start his own company—if he wants to, that is." The man then shook his head and left.

Joy chewed her lower lip. She wondered if she should call Rich and tell him how sorry she was. He must feel like someone adrift in the wide open sea. Her heart felt heavy just thinking about him. No, she'd already said it was over between them. She paced back and forth behind the cash register, feeling guilty for not calling him.

She felt nervous on Sunday afternoon as she drove to Mr. Bruce's estate. She spent all morning trying to think of something to tell Mr. Bruce to say to Rich on her behalf.

She had dressed in her most attractive sheath dress, and pulled her hair back into a bun. She felt she had to look professional when she went to a collector's house on business.

Joy drove down a long dirt road past acres of trees and fields. She let out a deep breath when she finally saw the large red brick colonial house.

Al Bruce came out to greet her before she even had a chance to get out of her car.

"Hi there," he called from the front door. "I'm glad you made it. We're ready for you, so come on inside." He then stepped away from the entrance to mumble something to someone unseen.

Joy wondered why he had said 'we.' He hadn't mentioned he was married or anything.

"Oh, your place is just lovely, Mr. Bruce." Joy said, looking around her as she got out of the car.

"Why, thank you. Call me Al, please. I hope you didn't have any trouble finding the place." He stepped forward to put a hand on her elbow.

"No, I didn't. I like drives through the countryside." When she entered the elaborate foyer, she couldn't take her eyes off the large wooden staircase. Several oil paintings hung on the stark white walls, and all of the furniture was antique.

Al Bruce motioned for her to follow him down the hall and then clapped his hands. "Well, I hope you're hungry. We're just setting up lunch in the dining room."

"We?" she asked.

"Yes, I hope you don't mind. I took the liberty of inviting my good friend to lunch. He's eager to see you." They walked into the large drawing room with French windows.

Joy gasped when she saw him. Rich Buckley

was standing in the corner of the room looking down at the keys of a grand piano. When he looked up and saw her, his mouth twitched. Slowly he began to smile, but she could not read the expression behind it. Was he really happy to see her, or was he just a bundle of nerves, as she was?

"Well, long time no see," he said after clearing his throat. "You look very well today, but then you always do." He smiled.

Al Bruce gestured for her to sit in one of the old wing chairs near the fireplace. He rubbed his hands together before taking a seat opposite her.

"Joy, let's just sit and relax for a few moments. I can show you my collection after lunch. Oh, I need to check on something first—I'll be right back," he said, springing from his chair.

After Al left the room, she turned to Rich. "Well, it's a big coincidence seeing you here."

"Actually, I just came over to visit Al today, and he said I should stay for lunch, and—"

"And just what did you tell him about me?" Joy interrupted with a snap, realizing she sounded much harsher than she intended.

"I've only ever told the truth about you, Joy." Rich sat down in the opposite wing chair and leaned forward. "I told him what a great shop you have and what a fair dealer you are." Then he paused before adding. "And what a marvelously different sort of woman you are." He leaned back in the chair and crossed his legs. "So tell me: how've you been?"

"I'm fine. I guess I should thank you for sending business my way." She quickly looked away from him; his presence felt too intense. She didn't know if she could handle looking into his eyes right now.

"Don't thank me," he answered, "it was nothing. Al knows lots about trains."

"Rich," Joy said, shifting her weight in her chair, "I'm so sorry you had to break up your company. I really am. Al told me all about it."

Rich just ran a hand through his hair. "Hey, it's no big loss. I didn't really like having Joe as a business partner anyway. I knew one day we'd probably part ways, but I felt I had to hold on because he'd started the business with Dad and all that." After rubbing his chin, he added, "I've been avoiding the Vouchers as much as possible lately."

Just then Al Bruce came back into the room and took a seat on the sofa opposite them. His face was bright with excitement. "Well, Miss Smathers, I do hope you like baked quail. That's what's being served for lunch today out in the dining room."

"Well, I thought your appraisal may take a while," Joy said with a puzzled expression. She noticed Rich was looking at the wall. Something felt odd.

"Yes, but come now, Miss Smathers. It's lunch time, and we really ought to eat first, I think. I'm hungry." Al Bruce was grinning from ear to ear as he glanced over at Rich.

Rich cleared his throat and stood up. Then he walked slowly to the other side of the room. Joy realized he couldn't hide how uncomfortable he was.

"Well, okay. But I hadn't really expected any-thing so formal."

Al Bruce let out a chuckle. "Dear me. I must confess—I like to do things in style. Don't I, Rich?"

Rich only swallowed and said nothing.

"So, Joy, tell me more about your background. I've always wondered how someone with a small business like yours is able to stay afloat these days. I mean, I know yours is a very unusual busi-ness." Al Bruce smiled, reddening in the face. It was obvious he was working hard to keep the con-versation going.

"So that woman bought those two Ronnie dolls, didn't she?" Rich asked, turning his head around.

Joy looked up. "Yes, she was thrilled to get them."

"I bet she was," Al Bruce said. "I don't know

much about dolls, but I know the very first Ronnie doll is a hard collectible to find."

An uncomfortable silence filled the room.

"Say, Joy, did you see this morning's paper?" Al asked, resting his elbow on his knee. "It's got a picture of Rich handing a check to the president of the National Cancer Foundation. He made a large donation in memory of Loretta Michaels. She was a friend of yours, wasn't she?"

Joy nodded and glanced at Rich, but his eyes would not meet hers. She could tell he wanted to say something but couldn't.

"Rich, that was generous of you." She was barely able to whisper the words.

"You should see it, Joy. It's a great picture of Rich here." Al Bruce turned to pick up a newspaper from the magazine rack near the sofa.

Before Joy could answer, Al said, "I really liked Mrs. Michaels. I know she had her share of problems in life, but I'm sure she was a decent person at heart."

"Oh yes, I loved her a lot." Joy replied.

"She was an important person in Joy's life, Al. She helped her open her shop," Rich interjected.

"Yes, yes," Al's expression turned serious. "I bet the foundation was probably overjoyed to get that money from the Ronnies' sale."

"Well, you know the money couldn't have been

given if Rich hadn't helped me locate those dolls."
Joy gazed down at the floor.

His back was still turned to her and he hadn't
looked at her once in the last ten minutes. She
wanted desperately to walk over and touch him,
but she didn't dare to do so in front of Al Bruce.
She wanted to know exactly what he was feeling
right now. His silence seemed to seep through her
soul and tell her he was troubled.

"Rich, I think they should do more for you than
just put your picture in the newspaper." Al threw
the paper onto the sofa arm and leaned back. "You
made a large donation, even though times aren't
so good for you right now."

"Right, Al. But. I'm not looking for any events
to be held in my honor. You know me better than
that." Rich slowly shifted his weight from foot to
foot and turned around.

"Yes. And I can tell, dear friend, from your
grumpy tone that you are getting hungry. So I
better go and see if lunch is ready to be served."
Al jumped to his feet and left the room.

Joy's body was trembling so much she could
feel the shivers run down her spine. She could not
look directly at Rich, even though part of her
wanted to be alone with him. She felt certain she
wouldn't know what to say to him. Her head was
spinning and she was unable to think clearly.

Just then a plump, middle-aged woman came in

and announced that lunch was ready to be served. She ushered everyone into the dining room.

Both Joy and Rich looked at Al as he said, "So, what do you two think?"

She kept re-arranging her napkin to fight her nerves. Both she and Rich were dead silent.

Why was she behaving like a shy schoolgirl? She had nothing to be embarrassed about. She had to confront this deep burning feeling. She couldn't keep avoiding her feelings forever. She knew she loved him; it was ridiculous to be so uncomfortable with someone you loved.

"I'm very eager to see your train sets, Al," she said before tasting a forkful of salad. "Even though dolls are my favorite toy, I do love train sets." She knew she was trying to chatter away the silence.

Neither one of the men answered her. They just looked at each other briefly and continued to eat.

"I'm sure you know all there is to know about trains from a collector's standpoint, Al. I mean, you probably have a very impressive collection. Just look at your house here—it's so lovely and well-decorated. I can't tell you how much I appreciate your hospitality." She cut into her quail and took a bite. "This is one of the best lunches I've had in a long while." She knew she probably sounded like an idiot chattering away like she was, but she couldn't stop. Neither man was look-

ing at her. "You know, I can't tell you how surprised I was to walk in and see Rich standing here.
I mean, it was a real shock." Then both of them
looked up at her from their plates. "I guess I
shouldn't have been that shocked; he is your
friend, after all."

She stopped and put her fork down. Now she
was talking too fast, and she wasn't making much
sense either. She felt this weird need to just ramble on.

"And I'm so glad you came in to my shop, Mr.
Bruce," she quipped.

Joy wanted to catch her breath, but then she
noticed the two men looking at each other. It
seemed there was some secret exchange between
the two of them. Neither was smiling. She turned
to look at Al Bruce at one end of the table.

"Mr. Bruce, let's go look at your train collection. I'm ready whenever you are," she said, pushing back her chair.

"Joy," Al said rising from his seat. "There's
something you should know. I don't really have
a train collection at all, just one old model I've
had since I was a kid. I actually purchased those
sets for Rich—he's the train lover, not me." He
paused. "But I think you already know that, don't
you?"

Rich lifted his head. His eyes met hers for a
lingering moment. Was there a plea on his face?

It suddenly dawned on her: he must have planned this entire appointment. He'd obviously wanted to see her.

Al Bruce cleared his throat and pushed his chair back into the table. "Well, I think I'd better leave the two of you alone for now. It appears you have a lot to discuss. I'll see you later."

Rich threw his napkin down and sat back in the chair. "No, Al, you haven't even finished your meal. Joy and I will go outside. We can talk out there." He pushed his chair back and stood up slowly. "Joy, will you please come outside with me?" he asked, extending his hand to her.

"Okay," she replied softly. "Thank you, Al."

"Well, I hope you two can work everything out," Al said as he sat back down.

Joy followed Rich outside. His hands were in his pockets and he was looking down at the ground as he walked.

"I'm sorry, Joy. I didn't know what to say to you for the longest time. I just felt I had to see you again. I've wanted to call you, but I've been too chicken. And I couldn't think of a way to get you to see me; I knew you were still angry."

She stood just a few feet away from him. The breeze was blowing through the tendrils of hair that hung loosely about her neck. She looked up at him, but his gaze was far away when he took a deep breath.

"You could've called me, Rich," she said, pushing the hair back from her face.

"I did contemplate going to your shop to talk to you, but I didn't think it was right, and I was ashamed of my attitude and behavior toward you. I also wasn't sure how to say what I want to say."

"And just what is it you want to say, Rich?" She looked at his handsome face as the wind tousled his dark hair.

"Joy, I haven't been able to stop thinking about you. You made me feel alive again, and you can't imagine what that feels like. A part of me died when Margie left me; I was too hurt to even think about closeness with anyone else again. I'm sorry if I embarrassed you at that party for Caroline. I just wanted her out of my life, and I wasn't thinking of your feelings at all. I didn't realize then what I do now." He shook his head sadly. "I see now that Caroline was so jealous because she picked up on what has only recently become obvious to me."

She moved closer to him, holding her breath.

He continued. "I've been so scared to say it, but I want you in my life. I never thought I could love again, but I love you enough to know my life from now on can be nothing without you. Here I stand before you without a secure future, but I just know we could grow together." He looked down at the ground. "So what do you say, Joy? Will you marry me?"

She reached up and put a hand to his cheek. Her heart was racing now, and she felt excitement in the crisp air.

"Rich," was all she could say.

"Joy, I need you as well as love you. You're the most lovable woman, and I'll treasure you and value you all the days of my life if you'll have me."

"I love you too, Rich Buckley. And, yes, I think I will grow to love you more as time goes by."

He pulled her to him. "We all make mistakes in life. Margie valued wealth and success over everything. Mrs. Michaels valued material possessions too much. We need to realize that relationships are the most important thing in life. I just knew I had to see you to tell you the truth about how I felt before it was too late for us."

"Oh Rich," Joy cried with happiness, falling into his arms.

He leaned over to kiss her forehead. "Now, how soon can we start planning our future together?"

Joy laughed. "We've got a lot of time to arrange that."

"Please say you'll marry me, Joy," he whispered.

She smiled and nodded her head. She then let

his mouth cover hers. The kiss was divine and loving. She never wanted it to end. There would be much in store for the future.

ANNOUNCEMENT:
MAINSTREET TRIBUNE

Mr. Rich Buckley, founder of the newly established and rapidly growing *Buckley Insurance Company*, married Joy Smathers, owner of *Joy's Lovable Collectibles* today in a quiet ceremony at town hall. Mrs. Cassie Fisher was the matron of honor, and Mr. Al Bruce was the best man.

Mr. Buckley is viewed by many in our community to be one of the few business leaders we have left concerned about quality of service. Joy Smathers Buckley is our town's leading expert on collectible toys.

Both exclaimed that they couldn't be happier.